"I Guess I Lose," Mariah Whispered. "But It Isn't Fair."

"The game is over, Mariah," Cash said. "Go to bed."

Without a word, Mariah abandoned her cards and began arranging her blankets for the night. After only a few moments she was ready for bed. She kicked out of her shoes and crawled into the cold nest she had made.

Cash stood up and moved around the cabin. Although Mariah tried not to watch him, it was impossible. Closing her eyes, she gripped the blankets tightly.

Suddenly her eyes snapped open. Cash was looming above her. "Cash?" she whispered.

His mouth settled over hers, stealing her breath. He drank deeply of her, holding the intimate kiss until her breathing was as broken and rapid as his own. Only then did he lift his head.

"You're right," he said hoarsely. "It isn't fair."

There was a rapid movement, then the sound of Cash climbing fully clothed into his sleeping bag.

It was a long time before either of them got to sleep.

Dear Reader:

Sensuous, emotional, compelling...these are all words that describe Silhouette Desire. If this is your first Desire novel, let me extend an invitation for you to sit back, kick off your shoes and revel in the pleasure of a tantalizing, fulfilling love story. If you're a regular reader, you already know that you're in for a real treat!

A Silhouette Desire can encompass many varying moods and tones. The story can be deeply moving and dramatic, or charming and lighthearted. But no matter what, each and every Silhouette Desire is a terrific romance written by and for today's woman.

I know you'll love March's *Man of the Month* book, *McAllister's Lady* by Naomi Horton. Also, look for *Granite Man*, one of Elizabeth Lowell's WESTERN LOVERS series. And don't miss wonderful love stories by some undeniable favorites *and* exciting newcomers: Kelly Jamison, Lucy Gordon, Beverly Barton and Karen Leabo.

So give in to Desire...you'll be glad you did!

All the best,

Lucia Macro
Senior Editor

ELIZABETH LOWELL

GRANITE MAN

SILHOUETTE *Desire*®

Published by Silhouette Books New York

America's Publisher of Contemporary Romance

For Lucia Macro,
who does a difficult job with grace

SILHOUETTE BOOKS
300 East 42nd St., New York, N.Y. 10017

GRANITE MAN

ISBN: 0-373-05625-4

First Silhouette Books printing March 1991

Printed in the U.S.A.

Books by Elizabeth Lowell

Silhouette Desire

Summer Thunder #77
The Fire of Spring #265
Too Hot to Handle #319
Love Song for a Raven #355
Fever #415
Dark Fire #462
Fire and Rain #546
Outlaw #624
Granite Man #625

Silhouette Intimate Moments

The Danvers Touch #18
Lover in the Rough #34
Summer Games #57
Forget Me Not #72
A Woman Without Lies #81
Traveling Man #97
Valley of the Sun #109
Sequel #128
Fires of Eden #141
Sweet Wind, Wild Wind #178
Chain Lightning #256

ELIZABETH LOWELL

is a pseudonym for Ann Maxwell, who also writes with her husband under the name of A.E. Maxwell. Her novels range from science fiction to historical fiction, and from romance to the sometimes gritty reality of modern suspense. All of her novels share a common theme—the power and beauty of love.

MACKENZIE FAMILY: WESTERN LOVERS

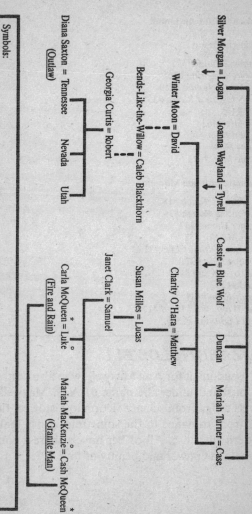

Silver Morgan = Logan

Joanna Wayland = Tyrell

Winter Moon = David

Bends-Like-the-Willow = Caleb Blackthorn

Georgia Curtis = Robert

Diana Saxton = Tennessee
(Outlaw)

Nevada

Utah

Cassie = Blue Wolf

Charity O'Hara = Matthew

Susan Milles = Lucas

Janet Clark = Samuel

Carla McQueen = Luke
(Fire and Rain)

Duncan

Mariah Turner = Case

Mariah MacKenzie = Cash McQueen
(Granite Man)

Symbols:

= literally "joins"
= Progeny of a formal union are shown with solid lines.

Dashed lines are illegitimate children.
* Carla and Cash McQueen are brother and sister.

° Mariah and Luke McKenzie are brother and sister.
↓ Family line continues

One

___

Forcing herself to let out the breath she had been holding, Mariah MacKenzie fumbled with the brass door knocker, failed to hang on to it, and curled her trembling fingers into a fist.

Fifteen years is a long time. I should have telephoned. What if my brother doesn't remember me? What if he throws me off the ranch? Where will I go then?

Using her knuckles, Mariah rapped lightly on the door frame of the ranch house. The sound echoed like thunder, but there was no response. She lifted her hand again. This time she managed to hold on to the horseshoe-shaped knocker long enough to deliver several staccato raps.

"Keep your shirt on! I'm coming!"

The voice was deep, impatient, unmistakably masculine. Mariah's heartbeat doubled even as she nervously took a backward step away from the door. A few instants later she was glad she had retreated.

The man who appeared filled the doorway. Literally. Mariah started to say her brother's name, only to find that her mouth was too dry to speak. She retreated again, unable to think, unable to breathe.

Cash McQueen frowned as he stared down at the slender girl who was backing away from him so quickly he was afraid she would fall off the porch. That would be a pity. It had been years since he had seen such an appealing female. Long legs, elegant breasts, big golden eyes, tousled hair that was the color of bittersweet chocolate, and an aura of vulnerability that slid past his hard-earned defenses.

"Can I help you?" Cash asked, trying to soften the edges of his deep voice. There was nothing he could do to gentle the rest of his appearance. He was big and he was strong and no amount of smiling could change those facts. Women usually didn't mind, but this one looked on the edge of bolting.

"My car b-boiled," Mariah said, the only thing she could think of.

"The whole thing?"

Cash's gentle voice and wry question drew a hesitant smile from Mariah. She stopped inching backward and shook her head. "Just the part that held water."

A smile changed Cash's face from forbidding to handsome. He walked out of the house and onto the front porch. Clenching her hands together, Mariah looked up at the big man who must be her brother. He had unruly, thick hair that was a gleaming chestnut brown where it wasn't streaked pale gold by the sun. He was muscular rather than soft. He looked like a man who was accustomed to using his body for hard physical work. His eyebrows were wickedly arched, darker than his hair, and his eyes were—

"The wrong color."

"I beg your pardon?" Cash asked, frowning.

Mariah flushed, realizing that she had spoken aloud.

"I'm—that is—I thought this was the Rocking M," she managed to stammer.

"It is."

All other emotions gave way to dismay as Mariah understood that the unthinkable had happened: the MacKenzie ranch had been sold to strangers.

Of the many possibilities she had imagined, this had not been among them. All her plans for coming back to the lost home of her dreams, all her half-formed hopes of pursuing a lost mine over the landscape of her ancestors, all her anticipation of being reunited with the older brother whose love had been the bright core of her childhood; all that was gone. And there was nothing to take its place except a new understanding of just how alone she was.

"Are you all right?" Cash asked, concerned by her sudden pallor, wanting to fold her into his arms and give her comfort.

Comfort? he asked himself sardonically. *Well, that too, I suppose. God, but that is one sexy woman looking like she is about to faint at my feet.*

A big, callused hand closed around Mariah's upper arm, both steadying her and making her tremble. She looked up—way up—into eyes that were a dark, smoky blue, yet as clear as a mountain lake in twilight. And, like a lake, the luminous surface concealed depths of shadow.

"Sit down, honey. You look a little pale around the edges," Cash said, urging her toward the old-fashioned porch swing. He seated her with a restrained strength that allowed no opposition. "I'll get you some water. Unless you'd like something with more kick?"

"No. I'm fine," Mariah said, but she made no move to stand up again. Her legs wouldn't have cooperated. Without thinking, she wrapped her fingers around a powerful, hairy wrist. "Did Luke MacKenzie—did the former owner leave a forwarding address?"

"Last time I checked, Luke was still the owner of the Rocking M, along with Tennessee Blackthorn."

Relief swept through Mariah. She smiled with blinding brilliance. "Are you Mr. Blackthorn?"

"No, I'm Cash McQueen," he said, smiling in return, wondering what she would do if he sat next to her and pulled her into his lap. "Sure you don't want some water or brandy?"

"I don't understand. Do you work here?"

"No. I'm visiting my sister, Luke's wife."

"Luke is married?"

Until Cash's eyes narrowed, Mariah didn't realize how dismayed she sounded. He looked at her with cool speculation in his eyes, a coolness that made her realize just how warm he had been before.

"Is Luke's marriage some kind of problem for you?" Cash asked.

Dark blue eyes watched Mariah with a curiosity that was suddenly more predatory than sensual. She knew beyond a doubt that any threat to his sister's marriage would be taken head-on by the big man who was watching her the way a hawk watched a careless field mouse.

"No problem," Mariah said faintly, fighting the tears that came from nowhere to strangle her voice. She felt her uncertain self-control fragmenting and was too tired to care. "I should have guessed he would be married by now."

"Who are you?"

The question was as blunt as the rock hammer hanging from a loop on Cash's wide leather belt. The cold steel tool looked softer than his narrowed eyes. The almost overwhelming sense of being close to hard, barely restrained masculinity increased the more Mariah looked at Cash—wide, muscular shoulders, flat waist, lean hips, long legs whose power was hinted at with each supple shift of his weight. Cash was violently male, yet his hand on her arm had been gentle. Keeping that in mind, she tried to smile up at him as she explained why she was no threat to his sister's marriage.

"I'm Mariah MacKenzie. Luke's sister." Still trying to smile, Mariah held out her hand as she said, "Pleased to meet you, Mr. McQueen."

"Cash." The answer was automatic, as was his taking of Mariah's hand. "You're Luke's *sister?*"

Even as Cash asked the question, his senses registered the soft, cool skin of Mariah's hand, the silken smoothness of her wrist when his grip shifted, and the racing of her pulse beneath his fingertips. Hardly able to believe what he had heard, he looked again into Mariah's eyes. Only then did he realize that he had been so struck by her sexual appeal that he had overlooked her resemblance to Luke. He, too, had tawny topaz eyes and hair so brown it was almost black.

But Mariah's resemblance to her brother ended there. All five feet, eight inches of her was very definitely female. Beneath the worn jeans and faded college T-shirt were the kinds of curves that made a man's hands feel both empty and hungry to be filled. Cash remembered the smooth resilience of her arm when he had steadied her, and then he remembered the warmth beneath the soft skin.

"What in hell brings you back to the Rocking M after all these years?"

There was no way for Mariah to explain to Cash her inchoate longings for a lost home, a lost family, a lost childhood. Each time she opened her mouth to try, no words came.

"I just wanted to—to see my brother," she said finally.

Cash glanced at his wrist. His new black metal watch told the time around the globe, was guaranteed to work up to a hundred and eighty feet underwater and in temperatures down to forty below zero. It was his third such watch in less than a year. So far, it was still telling time. But then, he hadn't been out prospecting yet. The repeated shock of rock hammer or pickax on granite had done in the other watches.

That, and panning for gold in the Rocking M's icy mountain creeks.

"Luke won't be in from the north range until dinner, and probably not even then," Cash said. "Carla is in Cortez shopping with Logan. They aren't due back until late tomorrow, which means that unless the Blackthorns get in early from Boulder, there won't be anyone to cook dinner except me. That's why I don't expect Luke back. Neither one of us would walk across a room to eat the other's cooking."

Mariah tried to sort out the spate of names and information, but had little success. In the end she hung on to the only words that mattered: Luke wouldn't be back for several hours. After waiting and hoping and dreaming for so many years, the hours she had left to wait seemed like an eternity. She was tired, discouraged and so sad that it was all she could do not to put her head on Cash's strong shoulder and cry. Her feelings were irrational, but then so was her whole hopeful journey back to the landscape of her childhood and her dreams.

It will be all right. Everything will work out fine. All I have to do is hang on and wait just a little longer. Luke will be here and he'll remember me and I'll remember him and everything will be all right.

Despite the familiar litany of reassurance Mariah spoke in the silence of her mind, the tears that had been making her throat raspy began to burn behind her eyelids. Knowing it was foolish, unable to help herself, she looked out across the ranch yard to MacKenzie Ridge and fought not to cry.

"Until then, someone had better go take a look at your car," Cash continued. "How far back down the road did it quit?"

He had to repeat the question twice before Mariah's wide golden eyes focused on him.

"I don't know."

The huskiness of Mariah's voice told Cash that she was fighting tears. A nearly tangible sadness was reflected in her tawny eyes, a sadness that was underlined by the vulnerable line of her mouth.

Yet even as sympathy stirred strongly inside Cash, bitter experience told him that the chances were slim and none that Mariah was one-tenth as vulnerable as she looked sitting on the porch swing, her fingers interlaced too tightly in her lap. Helpless women always found some strong, willing, stupid man to take care of them.

Someone like Cash McQueen.

Mariah looked up at Cash, her eyes wide with unshed tears and an unconscious appeal for understanding.

"I guess I'll wait here until . . ." Mariah's voice faded at the sudden hardening of Cash's expression.

"Don't you think your time would be better spent trying to fix your car?" Cash asked. "Or were you planning on letting the nearest man take care of it for you?"

The brusque tone of Cash's voice made Mariah flinch. She searched his eyes but saw none of the warmth that had been there before she had told him who she was.

"I hadn't thought about it," she admitted. "I didn't think about anything but getting here."

Cash grunted. "Well, you're here."

His tone made it clear that he was less than delighted by her presence. Fighting tears and a feeling of being set adrift, Mariah told herself that it was silly to let a stranger's disapproval upset her. She looked out toward the barn, blinked rapidly, and finally focused on the building. Its silhouette triggered childhood memories, Luke playing hide-and-seek with her, catching her and lifting her laughing and squirming over his head.

"Yes, I'm here," Mariah said huskily.

"And your car isn't."

"No." She banished the last of the memories and faced the big man who was watching her without pleasure. "I'll need something to carry water."

"There's a plastic water can in the barn."

"Is there a car I could drive?"

Cash shook his head.

Mariah thought of the long walk she had just made and was on the edge of suggesting that she wait for her brother's return before she tried to cope with her car. Cash's coolly appraising look put an end to that idea. She had received that look too many times from her stepfather, a man who took pleasure only in her failures.

"Good thing I wore my walking shoes," Mariah said with forced cheerfulness.

Cash muttered something beneath his breath, then added, "Stay here. I'll take care of it for you."

"Thank you, but that's not necessary. I can—"

"The hell you can," he interrupted abruptly. "You wouldn't get a hundred yards carrying two gallons of water. Even if you did, you wouldn't know what to do once you got there, would you?"

Before Mariah could think of a suitable retort, Cash stepped off the porch and began crossing the yard with long, powerful strides. He vanished behind the barn. A few minutes later he reappeared. He was driving a battered Jeep. As he passed the porch she realized that he didn't mean to stop for her.

"Wait!" Mariah called out, leaping up, sending the swing gyrating. "I'm going with you!"

"Why?" Cash asked, watching with disfavor as Mariah ran up to the Jeep.

"To drive the car back, of course."

"I'll tow it in."

It was too late. Mariah was scrambling into the lumpy passenger seat. Without a word Cash gunned the Jeep out of the yard and headed toward the dirt road that was the Rocking M's sole connection to the outer world.

The Jeep's canvas cover did little to shield the occupants from the wind. Hair the color of bittersweet chocolate flew in a wild cloud around Mariah's shoulders and whipped across her face. She grabbed one handful, then another, wrestling the slippery strands to a standstill, gathering and twisting the shining mass into a knot at the nape of her neck. As the wind picked apart the knot, she tucked in escaping strands.

Cash watched the process from the corner of his eye, intrigued despite himself by the glossy, silky hair and the curve of Mariah's nape, a curve that was both vulnerable and sexy. When he realized the trend of his thoughts, he was irritated. Surely by now he should have figured out that the more vulnerable a girl appeared, the greater the weapon she had to use on men such as himself—men who couldn't cure themselves of the belief that they should protect women from the harshness of life.

Stupid men, in a word.

"Luke didn't say anything about expecting you."

Although Cash said nothing more, his tone made it plain that he thought the ranch—and Luke—would have been better off without Mariah.

"He wasn't expecting me."

"What?" Cash's head swung for an instant toward Mariah.

"He doesn't know I'm coming."

Whatever Cash said was mercifully obliterated by the sudden bump and rattle as the Jeep hurtled over the cattle guard set into the dirt road. Mariah made a startled sound and hung on to the cold metal frame. The noise of wheels racing over the cattle guard, plus the smell of nearby grass and the distant tang of evergreens, triggered a dizzying rush of memories in Mariah.

Eyes the color of my own. Clever hands that made a doll whole again. Tall and strong, lifting me, tossing me, catching me and laughing with me. Dark hair and funny faces that made me smile when I wanted to cry.

There were other memories, too, darker memories of arguments and sobbing and a silence so tense Mariah had been afraid it would explode, destroying everything familiar. And then it had exploded and her mother's screams had gone on and on, rising and falling with the howling December storm.

Shivering in the aftermath of a storm that had occurred fifteen years ago, Mariah looked out over the hauntingly familiar landscape. She had recognized MacKenzie Ridge before she had seen the ranch buildings at its base. The rugged silhouette was burned into her memory. She had watched her home in the rearview mirror of her grandparents' car, and when the ranch buildings had vanished into a fold of land, she had sobbed her loss.

It hadn't been the house she mourned, or even the father who had been left behind. She had wept for Luke, the brother who had loved her when their parents were too consumed by private demons to notice either of their children.

That's all in the past. I've come home. Everything will be all right now. I'm finally home.

The reassuring litany calmed Mariah until she looked at the hard profile of the man who sat within touching distance of her. And she wanted to touch him. She wanted to ask what she had done to make him dislike her. Was it simply that she was alive, breathing, somehow reminding him of an unhappy past? It had been that way with her stepfather, an instant masculine antagonism toward another man's child that nothing Mariah did could alter.

What would she do if Luke disliked her on sight, too?

Two

Arms aching, Mariah held up the rumpled hood of her car while Cash rummaged in the engine compartment, muttering choice phrases she tried very hard not to overhear. A grimy, enigmatic array of parts was lined up on the canvas cloth that Cash had put on the ground nearby. Mariah looked anxiously from the greasy parts to the equally greasy hands of the big man who had taken one look at her sedan's ancient engine and suggested making a modern junk sculpture of it.

"When was the last time you changed the oil?"

The tone of voice was just short of a snarl. Mariah closed her eyes and tried to think.

"I can't remember. I wrote it in the little book in the glove compartment, but I needed paper for a grocery list so I—"

The rest of what Mariah said was lost beneath a rumble of masculine disgust. She caught her lower lip between her teeth and worried the soft flesh nervously.

"When was the last time you added water to the radiator?"

That was easy. "Today. Several times. Then I ran out."

Slowly Cash's head turned toward Mariah. In the shadow of the hood his eyes burned like dark, bleak sapphire flames. "What?"

Mariah swallowed and spoke quietly, calmly, as though gentleness and sweet reason was contagious.

"I always put water in the radiator every day, sometimes more often, depending on how far I'm going. Naturally I always carry water," she added, "but I ran out today. After that little town on the way in—"

"West Fork," Cash interrupted absently.

"That's the one," she said, smiling, encouraged by the fact that he hadn't taken her head off yet.

Cash didn't return the smile.

Mariah swallowed again and finished her explanation as quickly as possible. "After West Fork, there wasn't any place to get more water. I didn't realize how long it would take to get to the ranch house, so I didn't have enough water. Every time I stopped to let things cool off, more water leaked out of the radiator and I couldn't replace it, so I wouldn't get as far next time before it boiled and I had to stop. When I recognized MacKenzie Ridge I decided it would be faster to walk."

Shaking his head, muttering words that made Mariah wince, Cash went back to poking at the dirty engine. His hands hesitated as he was struck by a thought.

"How far did you drive this wreck?"

"Today?"

"No. From the beginning of your trip."

"I started in Seattle."

"Alone?"

"Of course," she said, surprised. Did he think she'd hidden a passenger in the trunk?

Cash said something sibilant and succinct. He backed out from beneath the hood, wiped his hands on a greasy rag and glared at the filthy engine; but he was seeing Mariah's lovely, uncertain smile, her clean-limbed, sexy body and her haunting aura of having been hurt once too often. He guessed that Mariah was a bit younger than his own sister, Carla, who was twenty-three. It made Cash furious to think of a girl who seemed as vulnerable as Mariah driving alone in a totally unreliable car from Seattle to the Rocking M's desolate corner of southwestern Colorado.

Cash took the weight of the hood from Mariah's hands and let the heavy metal fall into place with a resounding crash.

"What in hell were you thinking of when you set off across the country in this worthless piece of crud?"

Mariah opened her mouth. Nothing came out. She had driven the best vehicle she could afford. What was so remarkable about that?

"That's what I thought. You didn't think at all." Disgusted, Cash threw the greasy rag on top of the useless parts. "Well, baby, this wreck is D.O.R."

"What?"

"Dead on Road," Cash said succinctly. "I'll tow it to the ranch house, but the only way you'll get back on the road is with a new engine and you'd be a fool to spend that kind of money on this dog. From the wear pattern on the tires I'd guess the frame is bent but good. I know for damn sure the body is rusted through in so many places you could use it as a sieve. The radiator *is* a sieve. The battery is a pile of corrosion. The spark plugs are beyond belief. The carburetor—" His hand slashed the air expressively. "It's a miracle you got this far."

Mariah looked unhappily at the rumpled sedan. She started to ask if Cash were sure of his indictment, took one look at the hard line of his jaw and said nothing. Silently she watched while he attached her dead car to the Jeep. In spite of her unhappiness, she found herself appreciating the casual strength and coordination of his movements, a masculine grace and expertise that appealed to her in a way that went deeper than words.

Unfortunately, it was obvious to Mariah that the attraction wasn't mutual. After several attempts, she gave up trying to make small talk as she and Cash bumped down the one-lane dirt road leading toward the ranch house. Rather quickly the wind pulled apart the knot she had used to confine her hair. The silky wildness seethed around her face, but she didn't notice the teasing, tickling strands or the occasional, covert glances from Cash.

Mariah's long trip from Seattle in her unreliable car, her disappointment at not seeing Luke, her attraction to a man who found her aggravating rather than appealing—everything combined to drain Mariah's customary physical and mental resilience. She felt tired and bruised in a way she hadn't since her mother had died last year and she had been left to confront her stepfather without any pretense of bonds between them. Nor had her stepfather felt any need to pretend to such bonds. Immediately after the funeral, he had put a frayed cardboard carton in Mariah's hands and told her, *Your mother came to me with this. Take it and go.*

Mariah had taken the carton and gone, never understanding what she had done to earn her stepfather's coldness. She had returned to her tiny apartment, opened the carton, and found her MacKenzie heritage, the very heritage that her mother had refused ever to discuss. Holding a heavy necklace of rough gold nuggets in one hand, turning the pages of a huge family Bible with the other, Mariah had wept until she had no more tears.

Then she had begun planning to get back to the only home she had ever known—the Rocking M.

The Jeep clattered over the cattle guard that kept range cows from wandering out of the Rocking M's huge home pasture. Shrouded by dark memories, Mariah didn't notice the rattling noise the tires made as they hurtled over pipe.

Nor did Cash. He was watching Mariah covertly, accurately reading the signs of her discouragement. No matter how many times he told himself that Mariah was just one more female looking for a free ride from a man, he couldn't help regretting being so blunt about the possibilities of fixing her car. The lost look in her eyes was a silent remonstration for his lack of gentleness. He deserved it, and he knew it.

Just as Cash was on the verge of reaching for Mariah and stroking her hair in comfort, he caught himself. In silent, searing terms he castigated himself for being a fool. A child learned to keep its hands out of fire by reaching out and getting burned in the alluring dance of flames. A man learned to know his own weaknesses by having them used against himself.

Cash had learned that his greatest weakness was his bone-deep belief that a man should protect and cherish those who weren't as strong as himself, especially women and children. The weakest woman could manipulate the strongest man simply by using this protective instinct against him. That was what Linda had done. Repeatedly. After too much pain, Cash had finally realized that the more vulnerable a woman appeared, the greater was her ability to deceive him.

If the pain had gone all the way to the bone, so had the lesson. It had been eight years since Cash had trusted any woman except Carla, his half sister, who was a decade younger than he was and infinitely more vulnerable. From the day of her birth, she had returned his interest and his care with a generous love that was uniquely her own. Carla gave more than she received, yet she would be the first one to deny it. For that, Cash loved and trusted Carla, exempting her from his general distrust of the female of the species.

Wrapped in their separate thoughts, sharing a silence that was neither comfortable nor uneasy, Cash and Mariah drove through the home pasture and up to the ranch buildings. When he parked near the house, she stirred and looked at him.

"Thank you," she said, smiling despite her own weariness. "It was kind of you to go out of your way for a stranger."

Cash looked at Mariah with unfathomable dark eyes, then shrugged. "Sure as hell someone had to clean up the mess you left. Might as well be me. I wasn't doing anything more important than looking at government maps."

Before Mariah could say anything, Cash was out of the Jeep. Silently she followed, digging her keys from her big canvas purse. She unlocked the trunk of her car and was reaching for the carton her stepfather had given her when she sensed Cash's presence at her back.

"Planning on moving in?" he asked.

Mariah followed Cash's glance to the car's tightly packed trunk. Frayed cardboard cartons took up most of the space. A worn duffel crammed as full as a sausage was wedged in next to the scarred suitcase she had bought at a secondhand shop. But it wasn't her cheap luggage that made her feel ashamed, it was Cash's cool assumption that she had come to the Rocking M as a freeloader.

Yet even as Mariah wanted fiercely to deny it, she had to admit there was an uncomfortable core of truth to what Cash implied. She did want to stay on at the Rocking M, but she didn't have enough money to pay for room and board and fix her car, too.

The screen door of the ranch house creaked open and thudded shut, distracting Cash from the sour satisfaction of watching a bright tide of guilt color Mariah's face.

"Talk about the halt leading the lame," said a masculine voice from the front porch. "Are you towing that rattletrap or is it pushing your useless Jeep?"

"That's slander," Cash said, turning toward the porch. He braced his hands on his hips, but there was amusement rather than anger in his expression.

"That's bald truth," the other man retorted. "But not as bald as those sedan's tires. Surprised that heap isn't sitting on its wheel rims. Where in hell did you—" The voice broke off abruptly. "Oh. Hello. I didn't see you behind Cash. I'll bet you belong to that, er, car."

Mariah turned around and looked up and felt as though she had stepped off into space.

She was looking into her own eyes.

"L-Luke?" she asked hoarsely. "Oh, Luke, after all these years is it really you?"

Luke's eyes widened. His pupils dilated with shock. He searched Mariah's face in aching silence, then his arms opened, reaching for her. An instant later she was caught up in a huge bear hug. Laughing, crying, holding on to her brother, Mariah said Luke's name again and again, hardly able to believe that he was as glad to see her as she was to see him. It had been so long since anyone had hugged her. She hadn't realized how long until this instant.

"Fifteen years," Mariah said. "It's been fifteen years. I thought you had forgotten me."

"Not a chance, Muffin," Luke said, holding Mariah tightly. "If I had a dime for every time I've wondered where you were and if you were happy, I'd be a rich man instead of a broke rancher."

Hearing the old nickname brought a fresh spate of tears to Mariah. Wiping her eyes, smiling, she tried to speak but was able only to cry. She clung more tightly to Luke's neck, holding on as she had when she was five and he was twelve and he had comforted her during their parents' terrifying arguments.

"Without you, I don't know what would have happened to me," she whispered.

Luke simply held Mariah tighter, then slowly lowered her back to the ground. Belatedly she realized how big her brother had become. He was every bit as large as Cash. In fact, she decided, looking from one man to the other, they were identical in size.

"We're both six foot three," Luke said, smiling, reading his sister's mind in the look on her face. "We weigh the same, too. Just under two hundred pounds."

Mariah blinked. "Well, I've grown up, too, but not that much. I'm a mere five-eight, one twenty-six."

Luke stepped back far enough to really look at the young woman who was both familiar and a stranger. He shook his head as he cataloged the frankly feminine lines of her body. "Couldn't you have grown up ugly? Or at least skinny? I'll be beating men back with a whip."

Mariah swiped at tears and smiled tremulously. "Thanks. I think you're beautiful, too."

Cash snorted. "Luke's about as beautiful as the south end of a northbound mule. Never could understand what Carla saw in him."

Instantly Mariah turned on Cash, ready to defend her big brother. Then she realized that Luke was laughing and Cash was watching him with a masculine affection that was like nothing she had ever encountered. It was as though the men were brothers in blood as well as in law.

"Ignore him, Muffin," Luke said, hugging Mariah again. "He's just getting even for my comments about his ratty, unreliable Jeep." He looked over Mariah's head at Cash. "Speaking of ratty and unreliable, what's wrong with her car?"

"Everything."

"Um. What's right with it?"

"Nothing. She started in Seattle. It's a damned miracle she got this far. Proves the old saying—God watches over fools and drunks."

"Seattle, huh?" Luke glanced at the open trunk, accurately assessed its contents and asked, "Did you leave anything you care about behind?"

Mariah shook her head, suddenly nervous.

"Good. Remember the old ranch house where we used to play hide-and-seek?"

She nodded.

"You can live there."

"But . . ." Mariah's voice died.

She looked from one large man to the other. Luke looked expectant. Cash wore an expression of barely veiled cynicism. She remembered his words: *Planning on moving in?* Unhappily she looked back at Luke.

"I can't just move in on you," she said.

"Why not?"

"What about your wife?"

"Carla will be delighted. Since Ten and Diana started living part-time in Boulder, there hasn't been a woman for Carla to talk to a lot of the time. She hasn't said anything, but I'm sure she gets a little lonely. The Rocking M is hard on women that way."

Though Luke said nothing more, Mariah sensed all that he didn't say, their mother's tears and long silences, their father's anger at the woman who couldn't adjust to ranch life, a woman who simply slipped through his fingers into a twilight world of her own making.

"But I can't—" Mariah's voice broke. "I can't pay my way. I only have enough money for—"

Luke talked over her stumbling words. "Don't worry. You'll earn your keep. Logan needs an aunt and Carla sure as hell will need help a few months down the road. Six and a half months, to be exact."

The cynical smile vanished from Cash's mouth as the implication of Luke's words sank in.

"Is Carla pregnant?" Cash demanded.

Luke just grinned.

Cash whooped with pleasure and gave Luke a bone-cracking hug.

"It better be a girl, this time," Cash warned. "The world needs more women like Carla."

"I hear you. But I'll be damned grateful for whatever the good Lord sends along. Besides," Luke added with a wolfish smile, "if at first we don't succeed . . ."

Cash burst out laughing.

Mariah looked from one grinning man to the other and felt a fragile bubble of pleasure rise and burst softly within her, showering her with a feeling of belonging she had known only in her dreams. Hardly able to believe her luck, she looked around the dusty, oddly luminous ranch yard and felt dreams and reality merge.

Then Mariah looked at the tall, powerful man whose eyes were the deepest blue she had ever seen, and she decided that reality was more compelling than any dream she had ever had.

Three

___

"Are you sure you're a MacKenzie?" Cash asked Mariah as he removed another slab of garlic pork from the platter. "No MacKenzie I know can cook."

"Carla can," Luke pointed out quickly.

"Yeah, but that's different. Carla was born a Mc-Queen."

"And Mariah was born a MacKenzie," Nevada Blackthorn said matter-of-factly as he took two more slices of meat off the platter Mariah held out to him. "Even a hard-rock miner like you should be able to figure that out. All you have to do is look at her eyes."

"Thanks," Mariah said.

She smiled tentatively at the dark, brooding man whose own eyes were a startlingly light green. Nevada had been introduced to her as the Rocking M's *segundo,* the second in command. When his brother Ten was gone, Nevada was the foreman, as well. He was also one of the most unnerving men Mariah had ever met. Not once had she seen a smile flash behind his neatly trimmed beard. Yet she had no feeling that he disliked her. His reserve was simply part of his nature, a basic solitude that made her feel sad.

Cash watched Mariah smile at Nevada. Irritation pricked at Cash even as he told himself that if Mariah wanted to stub her toe on a hard piece of business like Nevada, it wasn't Cash's concern.

Yet no sooner had Cash reached that eminently reasonable decision when he heard himself saying, "Don't waste your smiles on Nevada. He's got no more heart than a stone."

"And you've got no more brain," Nevada said matter-of-factly. Only the slight crinkling at the corners of his eyes betrayed his amusement. "Like Ten says—Granite Man."

"Your brother was referring to my interest in mining."

"My brother was referring to your thick skull."

Cash grinned. "Care to bet on that?"

"Not one chance in hell. After a year of watching you play cards, I know why people nicknamed you Cash." Nevada glanced sideways at Mariah. "Never play cards with a man named Cash."

"But I like to play cards," she said.

"You do?" Cash asked, looking at her sharply.

Mariah nodded.

"Poker?"

Dark hair swung as Mariah nodded again.

"I'll be damned."

Nevada lifted one black eyebrow. "Probably, but not many men would brag about it."

Luke snickered.

Cash ignored the other men, focusing only on Mariah. It was easy to do. There was an elegance to her face and a subtle lushness to the curves of her body that caught Cash anew each time he looked at her. Even when he reminded himself that Mariah's aura of vulnerability was false, he remained interested in the rest of her.

Very interested.

"Could I tempt you into a hand or two of poker after dinner?" he asked.

"No!" Luke and Nevada said simultaneously.

Mariah looked at the two men, realized they were kidding—sort of—and smiled again at Cash. "Sure. But first I promised to show the MacKenzie family Bible to Luke."

An unreasonable disappointment snaked through Cash.

"Maybe after that?" Mariah asked hesitantly, looking at Cash with an eagerness she couldn't hide, sensing his interest despite his flashes of hostility. Though she had never been any man's lover, she certainly knew when a man looked at her with masculine appreciation. Cash was looking at her that way right now.

When Mariah passed the steaming biscuits to Cash, the sudden awareness of him that made her eyes luminous brought each of his masculine senses to quivering alert. Deliberately he let his fingertips brush over Mariah's hands as he took the warm, fragrant food from her. The slight catch of her breath and the abrupt speeding of the pulse in her throat told Cash how vividly she was aware of him as a man.

Covertly, Cash glanced at Luke, wondering how he would react to his sister's obvious interest in his best friend. Luke was talking in a low voice with Nevada about the cougar tracks the *segundo* had seen that morning in Wildfire Canyon. Cash looked back to Mariah, measuring the sensual awareness that gave her eyes the radiance of candle flames and made the pulse at the base of her soft throat beat strongly.

Desire surged through Cash, shocking him with its speed and ferocity, hardening him in an aching torrent of blood. He fought to control his torrential, unreasonable hunger for Mariah by telling himself that she was no better looking than a lot of women, that he was thirty-three, too old to respond this fast, this totally, to his best friend's sister. And in any case Mariah was just one more woman hungry for a lifetime sinecure—look at how quickly she had moved in on the Rocking M. Her token protests had been just that. Token.

"You're a good cook," Nevada said, handing Mariah the salt before she had time to do more than glance in the direction of the shaker. "Hope Luke can talk you into staying. From what Ten has told me, the Rocking M never had a cook worth shooting until Carla came along. But by January, Carla won't feel much like cooking."

"How did you know?" Luke asked, startled. "Dr. Chacon just confirmed it today."

Nevada shrugged. "Small things. Her skin. Her scent. The way she holds her body."

Cash shook his head. "Your daddy must have been a sorcerer. You have the most acute perceptions of anyone I've ever met."

"Chalk it up to war, not sorcery," Nevada said, pouring himself a cup of coffee. "You spend years tracking men through the night and see what happens to your senses. The Blackthorns come from a long line of warriors. The slow and the stupid didn't make the cut."

Nevada set the coffeepot aside and glanced back at Luke. "If you want, I'll check out that new cougar as soon as Ten gets back. I couldn't follow the tracks long enough to tell if it was male or female. Frankly, I'm hoping the cat is a young male, just coming out of the high country to mate and move on."

"I hope so, too. Wildfire Canyon can't support more than one or maybe two adult cats in a lean season. Long about February, some of the cattle in the upland pastures might get to looking too tasty to a big, hungry cat." Luke sipped coffee and swore softly. "I need to know more about cougars. The old ranchers say the cats are cow killers, the government says the cats only eat rabbits and deer. . . ." Frowning, Luke ran a hand through his hair. "Check into the new tracks when Ten comes back, but I can't turn you loose for more than a day or two. Too damned shorthanded."

"Need me?" Cash asked, trying and failing to keep the reluctance from his voice. He had been planning on getting in at least a week of prospecting in the Rocking M's high country. He no longer expected to find Mad Jack's lost mine, but he enjoyed the search too much to give it up.

"Maybe Luke needs you, but I don't," Nevada said. "When it comes to cows you make a hell of a good ranch mechanic."

Mariah looked at Cash and remembered his disgust with the state of her car's engine. "Are you a mechanic?"

Luke snickered. "Ask his Jeep. It runs only on alternate Thursdays."

"The miracle is that it runs at all," Nevada said. "Damned thing is even older than Cash is. Better looking, too."

"I don't know why I sit and listen to this slander," Cash complained without heat.

"Because it's that or do dishes. It's your turn, remember?" Luke asked.

"Yeah, but I was hoping you'd forget."

"That'll be the day." Luke pushed back from the table, gathered up his dishes and headed for the kitchen. "Nevada, you might want to stick around for the MacKenzie family show-and-tell. After all, some of them are your ancestors, too."

Nevada's head turned toward Luke with startling speed. "What?"

There was a clatter of dishes from the kitchen, then Luke came back to the big "mess hall" that adjoined the kitchen. He poured himself another cup of potent coffee before he looked down at Ten's younger brother with an odd smile.

"Didn't Ten tell you? The two of us finally figured it out last winter. We share a pair of great-great-grandparents— Case and Mariah MacKenzie."

"Be damned."

"No doubt," Cash said slyly, "but no man wants to brag about it, right?"

Nevada gave him a sideways glance that would have been threatening were it not for the telltale crinkling around Nevada's eyes. Luke just kept on talking, thoroughly accustomed to the masculine chaffing that always accompanied dinners on the Rocking M.

"Case was the MacKenzie who started the Rocking M," Luke explained as he looked back at Cash. "Actually, Mariah should have been one of your ancestors. Her granddaddy was a gold prospector."

"He was? Really?" Mariah said eagerly, her voice lilting with excitement. "I never knew that Grandpa Lucas was a prospector."

Luke blinked. "He wasn't."

"But you just said he was."

Simultaneously Nevada spoke. "I don't remember my parents talking about any MacKenzie ancestors."

"No, I didn't," Luke said to Mariah. Then, to Nevada, "I'm not surprised. It wasn't the kind of relationship that families used to talk about."

When Nevada and Mariah began speaking at once, Cash stood up with a resigned expression and began carrying dirty dishes into the kitchen. No one noticed his comings and goings or his absence when he stayed in the kitchen. Once he glanced through the doorway, saw Luke drawing family trees on a legal tablet and went back to the dishes. The next time Cash looked out, Mariah was gone. He was irrationally pleased that Nevada had remained behind. The bearded cowhand was too good-looking by half.

Cash attacked the counters with unusual vigor, but before he had finished, he heard Mariah's voice again.

"Here it is, Nevada. Proof positive that we're kissing kin."

The dishrag hit the sink with a distinct smack. Wiping his hands on his jeans, Cash moved silently across the kitchen until he could see into the dining room. Mariah stood next to Luke. She was holding a frayed cardboard carton as though it contained the crown jewels of England.

"What's that?" Luke asked, eyeing the disreputable box his sister was carrying so triumphantly to the cleared table.

"This is the MacKenzie family Bible," she said in a voice rich with satisfaction and subdued excitement.

There was a time of stretching silence ended by the audible rush of Luke's breath as Mariah removed the age-worn, leather-bound volume from the box. The Bible's intricate gilt lettering rippled and gleamed in the light.

Nevada whistled softly. He reached for the Bible, then stopped, looking at Mariah.

"May I?" he asked.

"Of course," she said, holding the thick, heavy volume out to him with both hands. "It's your family, too."

While Cash watched silently from the doorway, Nevada shook his head, refusing to take the book. Instead, he moved his fingertips across the fragile leather binding, caressing it as though it were alive.

The sensuality and emotion implicit in that gesture made conflicting feelings race through Cash—irritation at the softness in Mariah's eyes as she watched the unsmiling man touch the book, curiosity about the old Bible itself, an aching sense of time and history stretching from past to present to future; but most of all Cash felt a bitter regret that he would never have a child who would share his past, his present or his future.

"How old is this?" Nevada asked, taking the heavy book at last and putting it on the table.

"It was printed in 1867," Mariah said, "but the first entry isn't until the 1870s. It records the marriage of Case MacKenzie and Mariah Elizabeth Turner. I've tried to make out the date, but the ink is too blurred."

As she spoke, Mariah turned to the glossy pages within the body of the Bible where births, deaths and marriages were recorded. Finger hovering just above the old paper, she searched the list of names quickly.

"There it is," she said triumphantly. "Matthew Case MacKenzie, our great-grandfather. He married a woman called Charity O'Hara."

Luke looked quickly down the page of names, then pointed to another one. "And there's your great-granddaddy, Nevada. David Tyrell MacKenzie."

Nevada glanced at the birthdate, flipped to the page that recorded marriages and deaths, and found only a date of death entered. David Tyrell MacKenzie had died before he was twenty-six. Neither his marriage nor the births of any of his children had been recorded.

"No marriage listed," Nevada said neutrally. "No children, either."

"There wasn't a marriage," Luke said. "According to my grandfather, his uncle David was a rover and a loner. He spent most of his time living with or fighting various Indian tribes. No woman could hold him for long."

Nevada's mouth shifted into a wry line that was well short of a smile. "Yeah, that's always been a problem for us Blackthorns. Except for Ten. He's well and truly married." Nevada flipped the last glossy pages of the register, found no more entries and looked at Luke. "Nothing here. What makes you think we're related?"

"Mariah—no, not you, Muffin, the first Mariah. Anyway, she kept a journal. She mentioned a woman called Winter Moon in connection with her son David. Ten said your great-grandmother's name was Winter Moon."

Nevada nodded slowly.

"There was no formal marriage, but there was rumor of a child. A girl."

"Bends-Like-the-Willow," Nevada said. "My grandmother."

"Welcome to the family, cousin," Luke said, grinning and holding out his hand.

Nevada took it and said, "Well, you'll have no shortage of renegades in the MacKenzie roster now. The Blackthorns are famous for them. Bastards descended from a long line of bastards."

"Beats no descent at all," Luke said dryly.

Only Mariah noticed Cash standing in the doorway, his face expressionless as he confronted once again the fact that he would never know the sense of family continuity that other people took for granted. That, as much as his distrust of women, was the reason why he hadn't married again.

And why he never would.

Four

Cash turned back to the kitchen and finished cleaning it without taking time out for any more looks into the other room. When he was finished he poured himself a cup of coffee from the big pot that always simmered on the back of the stove and walked around the room slowly, sipping coffee. Finally he sat down alone at the kitchen table. The conversation from the dining room filtered through his thoughts, sounds without meaning.

His dark blue eyes looked at the kitchen walls where Carla had hung kitchen utensils that had been passed down through generations of MacKenzies and would be passed on to her own children. Cash's eyes narrowed against the pain of knowing that he would leave no children of his own when he died.

For the hundredth time he told himself how lucky he was to have a nephew whose life he was allowed to share. When he traced Logan's hairline and the shape of his jaw, Cash could see his own father and himself in his half-sister's child.

If Logan's laughter and curiosity and stubbornness made Cash ache anew to have a child of his own, that was too bad. He would just have to get over it.

"...real gold?"

"It is. The nuggets supposedly came from Mad Jack's mine."

Nevada's question and Mariah's answer were an irresistible lure for Cash. He set aside his cooled cup of coffee and went into the room that opened off the kitchen.

Mariah was sitting between Luke and Nevada, who was looking up from the handful of faded newspaper clippings and letters he had collected from the Bible. Despite his question, Nevada spared only a moment's glance for the gold that rippled and flowed between Mariah's hands like water. The necklace of nuggets linked by a long, heavy gold chain didn't interest Nevada as much as the faded, smudged marks on the brittle paper he held.

"Cash?" Luke called out without looking up. "What the hell is taking you so—oh, there you are. Remember the old jewelry I thought was lost? Look at this. Mother must have taken the chain when she left Dad. Muffin brought it back."

Cash's large, powerful hand reached over Mariah's shoulder. Her breath came in swiftly when his forearm brushed lightly against the curve of her neck and shoulder. His flesh was hard, radiating vitality, and the thick hair on his arm burned with metallic gold highlights. When he turned his hand so that it was palm up, Mariah saw the strong, raised, taut veins centered in his wrist, silent testimony to the times when his heart had had to beat strongly to feed the demands he made on his muscular body.

The sudden desire to trace the dark velvet branching of Cash's life was so great that Mariah had to close her eyes before she gave in to it.

"May I?" Cash asked.

Too shaken by her own reaction to speak, Mariah opened her eyes and handed the loops of chain over to Cash. She told herself it was an accident that her fingertips slid over his wrist, but she knew she lied. She also knew she would never forget the hard strength of his tendons or the alluring suppleness of the veins beneath the clean, tanned skin.

Silently Mariah watched Cash handle the necklace, testing its weight with his palm and the hardness of random nuggets with his fingernail. Very faint marks appeared on the rough gold, legacy of his skillful probing.

"High-test stuff," Cash said simply. "Damn few impurities. I couldn't tell without a formal assay, but I'd guess this is about as pure as gold gets without man's help."

"Is it from Mad Jack's mine?" Mariah asked.

Cash shrugged, but his eyes were intent as he went from nugget to nugget on the old necklace, touching, probing, measuring the malleable metal against his own knowledge and memories. Then, saying nothing, he took Mariah's hand and heaped the necklace in it. Gold chain whispered and moved in a cool fall over both sides of her palm, but the weight of the nuggets that remained in her palm kept the necklace from falling to the table.

Cash pulled a key from his jeans pocket. Dangling from the ring was a hollow metal cylinder about half the size of his thumb. With a deftness that was surprising for such big hands, he unscrewed the cylinder.

"Hold out your other hand," he said to Mariah.

She did, hoping that no one else sensed the sudden race of her heart when Cash's hand came up beneath hers, steadying it and cupping her fingers at the same time. Holding her with one hand, he upended the cylinder over her palm. She made a startled sound when a fat gold nugget dropped into her hand. The lump was surprisingly heavy for its size.

Carefully Cash selected a strand of chain and draped it over her palm so that one of the necklace nuggets rested next to the nugget he had taken from the cylinder. There was no apparent difference in the color of the gold, or in the texture of the surface. Both lumps of gold were angular and rough rather than rounded and smooth. Both were of a very deep, richly golden hue.

"Again, without an assay it's impossible to be sure," Cash said, "but . . ." He shrugged.

Mariah looked up at Cash with eyes the color of gold. "They're from Mad Jack's mine, aren't they?"

"I don't know. I've never found the mine." Cash looked down into Mariah's eyes and thought again of golden heat, golden flames, desire like a knife deep in his loins. "But I'd bet my last cent that these nuggets came from the same place, wherever that is."

"You mentioned that Case kept a journal," Mariah said, her voice a husky rasp that made Cash's blood thicken.

"Yes," Luke answered, though his sister hadn't looked at him, having eyes only for the gold in her hands—and for Cash, the man who hunted for gold.

"Didn't he say where the mine was?" she asked.

"No. All we know for sure was that Case had saddlebags full of gold from Mad Jack's mine."

"Why?"

"He was going to give it to Mad Jack's son. Instead he gave it to Mariah, Mad Jack's granddaughter."

That caught Mariah's attention. "You mean it's really true?" she asked, turning quickly toward Luke. "You weren't just joking? We're really related to Mad Jack?"

"Sure. Where else do you think the nuggets in that necklace came from? It used to be a man's watch chain. Mariah had it made for Case as a wedding gift. The chain came down through the family, staying with whichever son held the Rocking M. Until Mother left." Luke shrugged. "I guess she thought she had earned it. Maybe she had. God knows she hated every minute she ever spent on the ranch."

Mariah looked at the gold heaped on her palm, shining links infused with a legacy of both love and hatred. Yet all she said was "That explains the modern clasp. I assumed the old one had fallen apart, but watch chains don't need clasps, do they?" Without hesitation she poured the long, heavy chain and bulky nuggets into a heap in front of Luke. "Here. It belongs to you."

He looked startled. "I didn't mean—"

"I know you didn't," she interrupted. "It's still yours. It belongs with the man who holds the Rocking M. You."

"I've been thinking about that. Half of what I inherited should be—"

"No." Mariah's interruption was swift and determined. "The ranch was meant to be the inheritance of whichever MacKenzie son could hold it. Mariah's letters made that quite clear."

"That might have been fair in the past, but it sure as hell isn't fair now."

"It wasn't fair that our parents couldn't get along or that Mother had a nervous breakdown or that Dad drank too much or that I was taken away from the only person who really loved me. You." Mariah touched Luke's hand. "Lots of life isn't fair. So what?" Her smile was a bittersweet curve of acceptance. "You offered me a home when I had none. That's all I hoped for and more than I had any right to expect. Or accept."

"You'll by God accept it if I have to nail your feet to the floor," Luke said, squeezing Mariah's hand.

She laughed and tried to blink away the sudden tears in her eyes. "I accept. Thank you."

Luke picked up the gold chain and dumped it back in Mariah's hand. She tilted her palm, letting the heavy, cool gold slide back to the table.

"Mariah," he began roughly. "Damn it, it's yours."

"No. Make it back into a watch chain and wear it. Or give it to Logan. Or to your next child. Or to whichever child holds the Rocking M. But," Mariah added, speaking quickly, overriding the objections she saw in her brother's tawny eyes, "that doesn't mean I wouldn't like a gold necklace of my own. So, with your permission, I'll go looking for Mad Jack's mine. I've always believed I would find a lost gold mine someday.''

Luke laughed, then realized that Mariah was serious. Smiling crookedly, he said, ''Muffin, Cash has been looking for that mine for—how many years?''

''Nine.''

Startled, Mariah looked up at Cash. ''You have?''

He nodded slightly.

''And if a certified, multi-degreed geologist, a man who makes his living finding precious metals for other people—'' began Luke.

''You do?'' interrupted Mariah, still watching Cash with wide golden eyes.

He nodded again.

''—can't find Mad Jack's lost mine,'' Luke continued, talking over his sister, ''then what chance do you have?''

Mariah started to speak, then sighed, wondering how she could explain what she barely understood herself.

''Remember how you used to put me to bed and tell me stories?'' she asked after a few moments.

''Sure. You would watch me all wide-eyed and fascinated. Nobody ever paid that much attention to me but you. Made me feel ten feet tall.''

She smiled and said simply, ''You were. I would lie in bed and forget about Mother and Dad yelling downstairs and I'd listen to you talking about the calves or the new colts or some adventure you'd had. Sometimes you'd sneak in with cookies and a box full of old pictures and we would make up stories about the people. And sometimes you'd talk about Mad Jack and his mine and how we would go exploring and find it and buy everything the ranch didn't have so Mother would be happy on the Rocking M. We used to talk about that a lot.''

In silent comfort Luke squeezed Mariah's hand. ''I remember.''

She leaned forward with an urgency she couldn't suppress. "I've always believed I can find that mine. I'm Mad Jack's own blood, after all. Please, Luke. Let me look. What harm can there be in that?" Despite the need driving her, Mariah smiled teasingly and added, "I'll give you half of whatever I find, cross my heart and hope to die."

Luke laughed, shaking his head, unable to take her seriously. "Muffin, this is a big damned ranch. It's a patchwork quilt of outright ownership, plus lease lands from three government agencies, plus water rights and mineral rights and other things only a land lawyer or a professional gold hunter like Cash would understand."

"I'll learn."

"Oh hell, honey, if you found anything in Rocking M's high country land but granite and cow flops, I'd give it to you without hesitation and you know it, but—"

"Sold!" Mariah crowed, interrupting before Luke could say anything she didn't want to hear. She looked at Nevada and Cash. "You heard him. You're my witnesses."

Nevada looked up, nodded, and returned his attention to one of the old pieces of paper he held.

Cash was much more attentive to Mariah. "I heard," he said, watching her closely. "But just what makes you so sure that mine is on the Rocking M?"

"Mariah said it was. It's in her letter to the son who inherited the ranch."

Luke looked up at Cash. "You were right. Damn. I was hoping that mine would never..." He shrugged and said no more.

Silently Cash took the single nugget from Mariah's hand. A few deft movements returned the gold to its cylinder.

"What do you mean, Cash was right?" she asked. "And why were you hoping he was wrong?"

There was a pause before Luke said anything. When he finally did speak, he answered only her first question.

"When Mother cleaned out the family heirlooms, she overlooked a fat poke of gold, all that was left from Case's saddlebags. I showed the poke to Cash. He took one look and knew the gold hadn't come from any of the known, old-time strikes around here."

"Of course," Mariah said. "The MacKenzie gold wasn't found in placer pockets."

Cash looked at Mariah with renewed interest. "How did you know?"

"I did my homework." She held up her hand, ticking off names with her fingers. "The strikes at Moss Creek, Hard Luck, Shin Splint, Brass Monkey, Deer Creek, and Lucky Lady were all placer gold. Some small nuggets, a lot of dust. Everything was smooth from being tumbled in water." Mariah gestured toward the necklace. "For convenience we call those lumps of gold 'nuggets,' but I doubt they spent any real time in the bottom of a stream. If they had, they would be round or at least rounded off. But they're rough and asymmetrical. The longer I thought about it, the more certain I was that the lumps came from 'jewelry rock.'"

"What's that?" Luke asked.

Cash answered before Mariah could. "It's an old miner's term for quartz that is so thickly veined with pure gold that the ore can be broken apart in your bare hands. It's the richest kind of gold strike. Veins of gold like that are the original source of all the big nuggets that end up in placer pockets when the mother lodes are finally eroded away and washed by rain down into streams."

"Is that what you think Mad Jack's mine is?" Luke persisted. "A big strike of jewelry rock?"

"I wasn't sure. Except for the chunk you gave me—" Cash flicked his thumbnail against the cylinder "—the poke was filled with flakes and big, angular grains, the kind of thing that would come from a crude crushing process of really high-grade ore." Thoughtfully Cash stirred the chain with a blunt fingertip. Reflected light shifted and gleamed in shades of metallic gold. "But if these nuggets all came from Mad Jack's mine, it was God's own jewelry box, as close to digging pure gold as you can get this side of Fort Knox."

Luke said something unhappy and succinct beneath his breath.

Mariah looked at her brother in disbelief. "What's wrong with that? I think it's fantastic!"

"Ever read about Sutter's Mill?" he asked laconically.

"Sure. That was the one that set off the California gold rush in 1849. It was one of the richest strikes in history."

"Yeah. Remember what happened to the mill?"

"Er, no."

"It was trampled to death in the rush. So was a lot of other land. I don't need that kind of grief. We have enough trouble keeping pothunters out of the Anasazi ruins on Wind Mesa and in September Canyon."

"What ruins?" Mariah asked.

"They're all over the place. Would you like to see them?" Luke asked hopefully, trying to sidetrack her from the prospect of gold.

"Thanks, but I'd rather look for Mad Jack's mine."

Cash laughed ruefully. When he spoke, his voice was rich with certainty. "Forget it, Luke. Once the gold bug bites you, you're hooked for life. Not one damn thing is as bright as the shine of undiscovered gold. It's a fever that burns out everything else."

Luke looked surprised but Mariah nodded vigorously, making dark brown hair fly. She knew exactly what Cash meant.

Looking from Cash to Mariah, Nevada raised a single black eyebrow, shrugged, and returned his attention to the paper he was very gently unfolding on the table's surface.

"Smile," Mariah coaxed Luke. "You'd think we were talking about the Black Death."

"That can be cured by antibiotics," he shot back. "What do you think will happen if word gets out that there's a fabulous lost mine somewhere up beyond MacKenzie Ridge? A lot of our summer grazing is leased from the government, but the mineral rights *aren't* leased. There are rules and restrictions and bureaucratic papers to chase, but basically, when it comes to prospecting, it's come one, come all. Worst of all, mineral rights take precedence over other rights."

Mariah looked to Cash, who nodded.

"So we get a bunch of weekend warriors making campfires that are too big," Luke continued, "carrying guns they don't know how to use, drinking booze they can't hold, and generally being jackasses. I can live with that if I have to. What I can't live with is when they start tearing up the fences and creeks and watersheds. This is a cattle ranch, not a mining complex. I want to keep it that way."

"But..." Mariah's voice faded. She began worrying her lower lip between her teeth. "Does this mean I can't look for Mad Jack's mine?"

Luke swiped his fingers through his hair in a gesture of frustration. "No. But I want you to promise me two things. First, I don't want you telling anyone about Mad Jack's damned missing mine. That goes for Nevada, too. And I mean no one. Cash didn't even tell Carla."

"No problem," Nevada said. He looked at Cash with blunt approval. "You've been looking for nine years, huh? I like a man who can keep his mouth shut."

Cash's lips made a wry line and he said not one word.

"No problem for me, either," Mariah said, shrugging. "I don't have anyone to tell but you and you already know. What's the second thing?"

"I don't want you going out alone and looking for that damned mine," Luke said. "That's wild, rough country out there."

Mariah was on the verge of agreeing when she stopped. "Wait a minute. I can't tell anyone, right?"

Luke nodded.

"And you, Nevada and Cash are the only other ones who know. Right?"

"Carla knows," Luke said. "I told her myself."

"So five people know, including me."

"Right."

"Tell me, older brother—how much time do you have to spend looking for lost mines?"

"None," he said flatly.

"Nevada?"

He looked toward Luke, but it was Cash who spoke first.

"Nevada has cougar tracking duty. That takes care of his spare time for the summer."

The satisfaction in Cash's voice was subtle but unmistakable. Luke heard it. His smile was so small and swift that only Nevada saw it.

Mariah didn't notice. She was looking at Cash with hopeful eyes, waiting for him to volunteer. He didn't seem to notice her.

"No one prospects the high country in the winter," Luke said unhelpfully.

Mariah simply said, "Cash?"

"Sorry," he said. "That country is too rough for a tenderfoot like you."

"I've camped out before."

Cash grunted but was obviously unimpressed.

"I've hiked, too."

"Who carried your pack?"

"I did."

He grunted again. The sound wasn't encouraging.

Inspiration struck Mariah. "I'll do the cooking. I'll even do the dishes, too. Please?"

Cash looked at her luminous golden eyes and the graceful hand resting on his bare forearm in unconscious pleading. Desire shot through him at the thought of having her pleading with him for his skill as a lover rather than his expertise in hunting for gold.

"No," Cash said, more roughly than he had intended.

Mariah flinched as though she had been slapped. Hastily she withdrew her hand from his arm.

For an instant Luke's eyes widened, then narrowed with a purely male assessment. Soon his mouth shifted into a smile that was both sympathetic and amused as he realized what Cash's problem was.

"If I were you, Granite Man," Nevada drawled calmly, "I'd change my mind."

Cash shot the other man a savage look. "You're not me."

"Does that mean you're volunteering to go gold hunting?" Mariah said to Nevada, hoping her voice didn't sound as hurt as she felt by Cash's harsh refusal.

"Sorry, Muffin," Luke said, cutting across anything Nevada might have wanted to say. "I'm too shorthanded as it is. I can't afford to turn loose of Nevada."

"Damn shame," Nevada said without heat. "Hate to see a good treasure map go to waste."

"What?" Luke and Cash said together.

Silently Nevada pushed a piece of paper toward Mariah. Cash bent over her shoulder, all but holding his breath so that he wouldn't take in her fragile, tantalizing scent.

"I'm a warrior, not a prospector," Nevada said, "but I've read more than one map drawn by a barely literate man. Offhand, I'd guess this one shows the route to Mad Jack's mine."

Five

With a harshly suppressed sound of disgust and anger, Cash looked from the age-darkened, brittle paper to Mariah's innocent expression.

No wonder she was so eager to trade her nonexistent rights of inheritance in exchange for Luke's permission to prospect on the Rocking M—she has a damned map to follow to Mad Jack's mine!

Yet Mariah had looked so vulnerable when she had pleaded with Cash for his help.

Sweet little con artist. God. Why are men so stupid? And why am I so particularly stupid!

Mariah glanced from the paper to Nevada and smiled wryly. "I got all excited the first time I looked at it, too. Then I looked again. And again. I stared until I was cross-eyed, but I still couldn't make out two-thirds of the chicken scratches. Even if I assume Mad Jack drew this—and that's by no means a certainty—he didn't even mark north or south in any way I can decipher. As for labeling any of the landmarks, not a chance. I suspect the old boy was indeed illiterate. There's not a single letter of the alphabet on the whole map."

"He didn't need words. He read the land, not books." Nevada turned the map until the piece of paper stood on one chewed corner. "That's north," he said, indicating the upper corner.

"You're sure?" she asked, startled. "How can you tell?"

"He's right," Cash said an instant later. He stared at the map in growing excitement. "That's Mustang Point. Nothing else around has that shape. Which means . . . yes, there. Black Canyon. Then that must be Satan's Bath, which leads to the narrow rocky valley, then to Black Springs..." Cash's voice trailed off into mutterings.

Mariah watched, wide-eyed, as local place names she had never heard of were emphasized by stabs of Cash's long index finger. Then he began muttering words she had heard before, pungent words that told her he had run into a dead end. She started to ask what was wrong, but held her tongue. Luke and Nevada were standing now, leaning over the map in front of her, tracing lines that vanished into a blurred area that looked for all the world as though someone long ago had spilled coffee on the paper, blotting out the center of the map.

"Damn, that's enough to peeve a saint," Cash said, adding a few phrases that were distinctly unsaintly. "Some stupid dipstick smudged the only important part of the map. Now it's useless!"

"Not quite," Luke said. "Now you know the general area of the ranch to concentrate on."

Cash shot his friend a look of absolute disgust. "Hell, Luke, where do you think I've been looking for the past two years?"

"Oh. Devil's Peak area, huh?"

Cash grunted. "It's well named. It has more cracks and crannies, rills and creeks than any twelve mountains. It looks like it's been shattered by God's own rock hammer. I've used the line shack at Black Springs for my base. So far, I've managed to pan the lower third of a single small watershed."

"Find anything?"

"Trout," Cash said succinctly.

Mariah licked her lips. "Trout? Real, free-swimming, wild mountain trout?"

A smile Cash couldn't prevent stole across his lips. "Yeah. Sleek, succulent little devils, every one of them."

"Fresh butter, a dusting of cornmeal, a pinch of—"

"Stop it," groaned Cash. "You're making me hungry all over again."

"Does Black Springs have watercress?" she asked, smiling dreamily.

"No, but the creek does farther down the valley, where the water cools. Black Springs is hot."

"Hot? Wonderful! A long day of prospecting, a hot bath, a meal of fresh trout, camp biscuits, watercress salad...." Mariah made a sound of luxuriant anticipation.

Luke laughed softly. Cash swore, but there was no heat in it. He had often enjoyed nature's hard-rock hot tub. The meal Mariah mentioned, however, had existed only in his dreams. He was a lousy cook.

"Then you'll do it?" Mariah asked eagerly, sensing that Cash was weakening. "You'll help me look for Mad Jack's mine?"

"Don't push, Muffin," Luke said. "Cash and I will talk it over later. Alone."

"I'll give you half of my half," she said coaxingly to Cash, ignoring her older brother.

"Mariah—" began Luke.

"Who's pushing?" she asked, assuming an expression of wide-eyed innocence. "*Moi?* Never. I'm a regular doormat."

Nevada looked at Cash. "You need this map?"

"No."

"Then if nobody minds, I'd like to pass it along to some people who are real good at making ruined documents give up their secrets."

Cash started to ask questions, then remembered where—and for whom—Nevada had worked before he came to the Rocking M.

"Fine with me," Cash said. "The map belongs to Luke and Mariah, though."

"Take it," said Luke.

"Sure. Who are you sending it to?" Mariah asked.

"Don't worry. They'll take good care of it," Nevada said, folding the map delicately along age-worn creases.

"But where are you sending it?"

Mariah was talking to emptiness. Nevada had simply walked away from the table. The back door opened and closed quietly.

"I didn't mean to make him mad."

"You didn't," Luke said, stretching. "Nevada isn't long on social niceties like smiling and saying excuse me. But he's a damned good man. One of the best. Just don't ever push him," Luke added, looking directly at Cash. "Even you. Nevada doesn't push worth a damn."

Cash smiled thinly. "My mother didn't hatch any stupid chicks. I saw Nevada fight once. If I go poking around in that lion's den, it will be with a shotgun."

"But where is Nevada taking the map?" Mariah asked in a plaintive voice.

"I don't know," Luke admitted. "I do know you'll get it back in as good shape as it was when Nevada took it. Better, probably."

"Then you must know where he's taking it."

"No, but I can make an educated guess."

"Please do," Mariah said in exasperation.

Luke smiled. "I'd guess that map will end up in an FBI lab on the east coast. Or some other government agency's lab. Nevada wasn't always a cowboy." Luke stretched and yawned again, then looked at Mariah. "Did you get everything moved into the old house?"

"Yes."

"All unpacked?"

"Well, not quite."

"Why don't you go finish? I'll be along in a few minutes to make sure you have everything you need."

"Why do I feel like I'm being told to leave?"

"Because you are."

Mariah started to object before she remembered that Luke wanted to talk with Cash in private about going prospecting with her.

"I'm not six years old anymore," she said reasonably. "You can talk in front of me."

It was as though she hadn't spoken.

"Don't forget to close the bathroom window," Luke said, "unless you want a battle-scarred old tomcat sleeping on your bed."

Mariah looked at Cash. "Why do you let him insult you like that?"

There was a two-second hesitation before Cash laughed out loud, but the sudden blaze in his eyes made Mariah's heart beat faster.

Shaking his head, Luke said, "Good night, Muffin."

"Don't forget to bring my cookies and milk," she retorted sweetly, "or I'll cry myself to sleep."

Luke grabbed Mariah, hugged her and ruffled her hair as though she were six years old again. Laughing, she stood on tiptoe and returned the favor, then found herself suddenly blinking back tears.

"Thank you, Luke," she said.

"For what?"

"Not throwing me out on my ear when I turned up without warning."

"Don't be silly. This is your home."

"No," she whispered, "it's yours. But I'm grateful to share it for a while."

Before Luke could say anything else, she kissed his cheek and walked quickly from the dining room. Cash stood and watched the outer door for a long, silent moment, admiring the perfection with which Mariah played the role of vulnerable child-woman. She was very good. Even better than Linda had been, and Linda had fooled him completely. Of course, Linda had had a real advantage. She had told him something he would have sold his soul to believe—that she was carrying his child.

What he hadn't known until too late was that Linda had been sleeping with another man. That was another thing women were good at—making each man feel like he was the only one.

"You don't have to worry about Nevada," Luke said calmly.

Startled, Cash turned toward his friend. "What do you mean?"

"Oh, he's a handsome son, but it's you Mariah keeps looking at." Deadpan, Luke added, "Which proves that there's no accounting for taste."

"Despite the beard, Nevada isn't a prospector," Cash pointed out coolly, "and the lady's heart is obviously set on gold."

"The lady was looking at you before she knew you were a prospector. And you were looking at her, period."

Cash's eyes narrowed into gleaming slits of blue. Before he could say anything, Luke was talking again.

"Yeah, yeah, I know, it puts a man between a rock and a hard place when he wants his best friend's little sister. Hell, I ought to know. I spent a lot of years wanting Carla."

"Not as many as she spent wanting you."

Luke smiled crookedly. "So I was a prize fool. If it weren't for her matchmaking older brother, I'd still be waking up alone in the middle of the night."

"Is that what you're doing now? Matchmaking? Is that why you want me to go prospecting with Mariah? You figure we'll find something more valuable and permanent than gold?"

Wincing at Cash's sardonic tone, Luke raked his fingers through his hair as he said, "The area around Devil's Peak is damned wild country."

Cash looked at the ceiling.

"I can't let her go alone," Luke continued.

Cash looked at his hands.

"I can't take her myself."

Cash looked at the floor.

"I need every cowhand I've got, and five more besides."

Cash looked at the table.

Luke swore. "Forget it. I'll get Nevada to—"

"Hell," Cash interrupted fiercely, angered by the thought of throwing Mariah and Nevada together in the vast, lonely reaches of the Rocking M's high country. Cash pinned Luke with a black look. "All right, I'll do it. But I'm usually gone for weeks at a time. Have you thought about that?"

"Mariah said she was a camper. Besides, there's always the Black Springs line shack."

"Damn it, that's not what I mean and you know it! Your sister is one very sexy female."

Luke cocked his head to one side. "Interesting."

A snarl was Cash's only answer.

"No, I mean it," Luke continued. "Not that I think Mariah is a dog, but sexy wouldn't be the word I'd use to describe her. Striking, maybe, with those big golden eyes and lovely smile. Warm. Quick. But not sexy."

"I wouldn't describe Carla as sexy, either."

"Then you're blind."

"No. I'm her brother."

"Point taken," Luke said, grinning.

There was silence, then Cash spoke in a painfully reasonable tone of voice. "Look. It takes half a day just to get to the Black Springs line shack by horseback. From there, it's a hard scramble up boulder-choked creeks and steep canyons. There's no way we can duck in, poke around for a few hours, and duck out. We'll be spending a lot of nights alone."

"I trust you."

"Then you are a damned fool," Cash said, spacing each word carefully.

"You trusted me in the wilds of September Canyon with Carla," Luke pointed out.

"Yeah. Think about it. Carla ended up pregnant and alone."

Luke grimaced. "You're not as big a fool as I was."

"Damn it—"

"Mariah is twenty-two," Luke continued over Cash's words, "college educated, a consenting adult in every sense of the word. I trust you in exactly the same way you trusted me, and for the same reason. You may be hardheaded as hell and not trust women worth a damn, but you would never touch a girl unless she wanted you to. Mariah will never be safer in that way than when she is with you. Beyond that, whatever happens or doesn't happen between the two of you is none of my business."

For a minute there was no sound in the dining room. Cash stood motionless, his hands jammed in his back pockets, his mind racing as he assessed the situation and the man he loved more than most men loved their blood brothers. In the end, there was only one possible conclusion: Luke meant every word he had said.

Well, at least I won't have to worry about getting Mariah pregnant the way Luke did Carla.

But Cash's bitterly ironic thought remained unspoken. It wasn't the sort of thing a man talked about.

"I'll hold you to that," Cash said finally.

Luke nodded, then smiled widely and gave Cash an affectionate whack on his shoulder. "Thanks for getting me off the hook. I owe you one."

"Like hell. I spend more time here than I do in my apartment in Boulder."

"So move here. You can build at the other end of the big pasture, just across the stream from Ten and Diana. Plenty of space."

"One of these days you're going to say that and I'm going to take you up on it."

"Why do you think I keep saying it?" Luke stretched and yawned. "Damn, I wish Carla were home. I never sleep as well when she's gone."

"You're breaking my heart. Go to bed."

"Mariah's waiting for me."

"I'll tell her what we decided," Cash said. "With luck, she'll change her mind when she finds out Nevada won't be her trusty wilderness guide."

"Are you deaf as well as blind? I keep telling you, it's not Nevada she's looking at!"

Cash turned on his heel and left the room without saying another word, but he let the outside door close behind him hard enough to make a statement about his temper.

Outside, the cool summer darkness was awash with stars and alive with the murmur of air sliding down from the highlands to the long, flat valley that was the Rocking M's center. Lights burned in the bunkhouse and in the old ranch house. Cash moved with the swift, ground-covering strides of a man who has spent much of his adult life walking over wild lands in search of the precious metals that fed civilization's endless demands. Though he wore only a shirt and jeans, he didn't notice the crisp breeze. He knocked on the front door of the old ranch house with more force than courtesy.

"Come in, Luke. It's open."

"It's Cash. Is it still open?"

Mariah looked down at her oversize cotton nightshirt and bare feet. For an instant she wished she were wearing Spanish lace, Chinese silk and French perfume. Then she sighed. As angry as Cash sounded, she could be naked and it wouldn't make a speck of difference.

What is it about me that irritates him?

There was no answer to the question, other than the obvious one. He wasn't wild about the idea of being saddled with her out in the backcountry, just as he hadn't been wild about helping her with her car. He looked at her as a helpless, useless burden. That shouldn't surprise her. Her stepfather had felt precisely the same way.

Mariah opened the door and stifled an impulse to slam it shut before Cash could come in. He towered over her, looming out of the darkness like a mountain, and his eyes were black with anger.

"Come in, or would you rather bite my head off out in the yard?"

The sound Cash made could most politely be described as a growl. He stepped forward. Mariah retreated. A gust of wind sucked the door shut.

Cash looked at the nightshirt that should have concealed Mariah's curves but ended up teasing him by draping softly over her breasts and hips. Desire tightened his whole body, hammering through him with painful intensity. The thought of being alone with her night after night was enough to make him slam his fist into the wall from sheer frustration.

"What do you know about wild country?" Cash asked savagely.

"It's where gold is found."

He hissed a single word, then said, "This won't be a trendy pseudo-wilderness trek along a well-beaten path maintained by the National Park Service. Can you even ride a horse?"

"Yes."

"Can you ride rough country for half a day, then scramble over rocks for another half day?"

"If I have to."

"The line shack leaks and it rains damn near every night. The only privy is a short-handled shovel. At the end of a hard day you have to gather firewood, haul water, wash out your socks so you won't blister the next day, eat food you're too tired to cook properly, sleep on a wood floor that has more drafts than bare dirt would and—"

"You make it sound irresistible," Mariah interrupted. "I accept."

"Damn it, you aren't even listening!"

"You aren't telling me anything I don't already know."

"Then you better know this. We'll be alone out there, and I mean *alone*."

Mariah met Cash's dark glance without flinching and said, "I've been alone since I was dragged off the Rocking M fifteen years ago."

Cash jammed his hands into his back pockets. "That's not what I meant, lady. Up on Devil's Peak you could scream your pretty head off and no one would hear."

"You would."

"What if I'm the one making you scream? Have you thought about that?"

"Frankly, you're making me want to scream right now."

There was a charged silence.

Mariah smiled tentatively and put her hand out in silent appeal. "I know what you're trying to say, Cash, but let's be honest. I don't have the kind of looks that drive a man crazy with desire and we both know it. Just as we both know you don't want to take me across the road, much less spend a few weeks in the wild with me. But I'm going to Devil's Peak. I've been dreaming of looking for Mad Jack's mine as long as I can remember. Come hell or high water, that's what I'm going to do."

Cash looked down at the pale, graceful hand held out to him in artful supplication. He remembered how cool and silky Mariah's fingers had felt when they had rested on his bare forearm. He remembered how quickly her hand had warmed at his touch. He wondered if all of her would catch fire that fast.

The thought made him burn.

"I'll take care of packing the supplies and horses," Cash said coldly, "because sure as hell you won't know how. We leave in five hours. If you aren't ready, I'll leave without you."

"I'll be ready."

Cash turned and left the house before Mariah could see just how ready he was right now.

Six

Five hours later Mariah pulled open the front door before Cash could knock. Silently he stared at her, noting the lace-up shoes, faded jeans, an emerald turtleneck T-shirt beneath a black V-necked sweater and a long-sleeved man's flannel shirt that ended at her hips. The arms of a windbreaker were tied casually around her neck. The outfit should have made her look as appealing as a mud post, but it was all he could do not to run his hands over her to find the curves he knew waited beneath the sensible trail clothes.

"Here," Cash said, holding out a pair of cowboy boots. "Luke said to wear these if they fit. They're Carla's."

While Mariah tried on the boots, Cash glanced around. She had packed a lot less gear than he had expected. A military surplus backpack was stuffed tightly and propped against the wall. Other military surplus items were tied to the backpack—canteen, mess kit and the like. Extra blankets had been rolled up and tied with thongs.

"Where's your sleeping bag?" he asked.

"I don't have one."

"What the hell are you planning to sleep on?"

"My side, usually. Sometimes my stomach."

Cash clenched his jaw. "What about hiking boots?"

"My shoes are tougher than they look." Mariah stood and stamped her feet experimentally. "They're long enough, but they pinch in the toes."

"That's how you know they're cowboy boots," Cash retorted.

Mariah glanced at Cash's big feet. He was wearing lace-up, rough-country hiking boots that came to just below his knees. The heels were thick enough to catch and hold the edge of a stirrup securely. She had priced a similar pair in Seattle and decided that she would have to find Mad Jack's mine before she could afford the boots.

She bent down, tied her shoes to the backpack, and picked it up. "Ready."

Cash's long, powerful arm reached out, snagged Mariah's impromptu bedroll, and stuffed it none too gently into her hands. "Don't forget this."

"You're too kind," she muttered.

"I know."

Empty-handed, Cash followed Mariah to the corral. Four horses waited patiently in the predawn darkness. Two of them were pack animals. The other two were saddled. Cash added Mariah's scant baggage to one of the existing packs and lashed everything securely in place. Moments later he stepped into the saddle of a big, rawboned mountain horse, picked up the lead rope of the pack animals and headed out into the darkness without so much as a backward look.

"It won't work," Mariah said clearly. "I don't need your help to carry my stuff. I don't need your help to get on a horse. I don't need your help for one damned thing except to make Luke feel better!"

If Cash heard, he didn't answer.

Mariah went to the remaining horse, untied it and mounted a good deal less gracefully than Cash had. It had been six years since she had last ridden, but the reflexes and confidence were still there. When she reined the small mare around and booted it matter-of-factly in the ribs, it quickly trotted after Cash's horse. The mare was short-legged and rough-gaited, but amiable enough for a child to ride.

An hour later Mariah would have traded the mare's good temperament for a mean-spirited horse with a trot that didn't rattle her teeth. The terrain went up and down. Steeply. If there was a trail, Mariah couldn't make it out in the darkness, which meant that she spent a lot of time slopping around in the saddle because there was no way for her to predict her horse's next movements. She would be lucky to stand up at the end of three more hours of such punishment, much less hike with a backpack up a steep mountain and look for gold until the sun went down.

Don't forget the bit about hauling water and washing your socks, Mariah advised herself dryly. *On second thought, do forget it. No socks could be that dirty.*

When dawn came, it was a blaze of incandescent beauty that Mariah was too uncomfortable to fully appreciate. Whichever way she turned in the saddle, her body complained.

Even so, she felt the tug of undiscovered horizons expanding away in all directions. It was exciting to be in a place where not so much as a glimpse of man was to be seen. For all that she could tell, she and Cash might have been the first people ever to travel the land. Wild country rolled away from her on all sides in pristine splendor, shades of green and white and gray, evergreens and granite.

Mixed in with the darker greens of conifers was the pale green of aspens at the higher elevations, a green that was subtly repeated by grassy slopes at the lower elevations and occasional meadows in between. Ahead, Devil's Peak loomed in black, shattered grandeur, looking like the eroded ruins of a volcano rather than the granite peak Mariah had expected.

I wonder why Cash is searching for gold on a volcano's flanks? All the strikes I've read about were in granite, not lava.

Mariah would have asked Cash to explain this reasoning to her, but she had promised herself that she wouldn't speak until he did. Not even to ask for a rest break. Instead, she just hooked one leg around the saddle horn and rode side-saddle for a time. She prayed there would be enough strength left in her cramped muscles to keep her upright after she dismounted.

As the sun rose, its heat intensified until it burned through the high country's crystalline air. The last chill of night quickly surrendered to the golden fire. Mariah began shedding layers of clothing until only the long-sleeved, fitted ski shirt remained. She unzipped the turtleneck collar and shoved up the sleeves, letting the breeze tease as much of her skin as it could reach.

At the end of four hours, Mariah rather grimly reined the mare down a narrow rocky crease that opened into a tiny valley. Although Cash had been only a few minutes ahead of her, he had already unloaded the pack animals and was in the act of throwing his saddle over the corral railing. Even as Mariah resented it, she envied his muscular ease of movement. She pulled her horse to a halt and slowly, carefully, began to dismount.

Two seconds later she was sitting in the dirt. Her legs simply hadn't been able to support the rest of her. She gritted her teeth and was beginning the tedious job of getting to her feet when she felt herself picked up with dizzying speed. The world shifted crazily. When it settled again, she was being carried like a child against Cash's chest.

"I thought you said you could ride," Cash said harshly.

"I can." Mariah grimaced. "I just proved it, remember?"

"And now you won't be able to walk."

"*Quelle* shock. Wasn't that the whole idea? You didn't want me looking for gold with you and now I won't be able to. Not right away, at any rate. I'll be fine as soon as my legs start cooperating again and then you'll be out of luck."

Cash's mouth flattened into a hard line. "How long has it been since you were on a horse?"

"About a minute."

Against his will, Cash found himself wanting to smile. Any other woman would have been screaming at him or crying or doing both at once. Despite the grueling ride, Mariah's sense of humor was intact. Biting, but intact.

And she felt exciting in his arms, warm and supple, soft, fitting him without gaps or angles or discomfort. He shifted her subtly, savoring the feel of her, silently urging her to relax against his strength.

"Sorry, honey," he said. "If I had known how long it had been since—"

"Pull my other leg," Mariah interrupted. Then she smiled wearily. "On second thought, don't. It might fall off."

"How long has it been since you've ridden?" he asked again.

"Years. Six blessed, wonderful years."

Cash said something savage.

"Oh, it's not that bad," Mariah said.

"You sure?"

"Yeah. It's worse."

He laughed unwillingly and held her even closer. She braced herself against the temptation to put her head on the muscular resilience of his chest and relax her aching body. Her head sagged anyway. She sighed and gave herself to Cash's strength, figuring he had plenty to spare.

"A soak in the hot springs will help," he said.

Mariah groaned softly at the thought of hot water drawing out the stiffness of her muscles.

"My swimsuit is in my backpack," she said. "Better yet, just give me a bar of soap and throw me in as is. That way I won't have to haul water to wash my socks."

Laughing soundlessly, shaking his head, Cash held Mariah for a long moment in something very close to a hug. She might be an accomplished little actress in some ways, but she was good company in others. Linda hadn't been. When things didn't go according to her plan—and often even when they did—she pouted and wheedled like a child after candy. At first it had been gratifying to be the center of Linda's world. Gradually it had become tedious to be cast in a role of father to a manipulative little girl who would never grow up.

A long, almost contented sigh escaped Mariah's lips, stirring the hair that pushed up beneath Cash's open collar. A visible ripple of response went through him as he felt her breath wash over his skin. He clenched his jaw and walked toward the corral fence.

"Time to stand on your own two feet," he said tightly.

With the unself-consciousness of a cat, Mariah rubbed her cheek against Cash's shirt and admitted, "I'd rather stand on yours."

"I figured that out the first time I saw you."

The sardonic tone of Cash's voice told Mariah that the truce was over. She didn't know what she had done to earn either the war or the truce. All she knew was that she had never enjoyed anything quite so much as being held by Cash, feeling the flex and resilience of his body, being so close to him that she could see sunlight melt and run through his hair like liquid gold.

When Cash's left arm released Mariah's legs, everything dipped and turned once more, but slowly this time. Instinctively she put her arms around his neck, seeking a stable center in a shifting world. Held securely more by the hard power of his right arm than by both her own arms, Mariah felt her hips slide down the length of Cash's body with a slow intimacy that shook her. Her glance flew to his face. His expression was as impassive as granite.

"Grab hold of the top rail," Cash instructed.

Mariah reached for the smooth, weathered wood with a hand that trembled. As she twisted in Cash's arms, the fitted T-shirt outlined her breasts in alluring detail, telling of the soft, feminine flesh beneath.

He wondered whether her nipples were pink or dusky rose or even darker, a vivid contrast to the pale satin of her skin. He thought of bending down and caressing her breasts with his tongue and teeth, drawing out the nipples until they felt like hot, hard velvet and she twisted beneath him, crying for release from the passionate prison of their lovemaking.

Don't be a fool, Cash told himself savagely. *No woman ever wants a man like that. Not really. Not so deep and hard and wild she forgets all the playacting, all the survival calculations, all the cunning.*

Yet, despite the cold lessons of past experience, when Cash looked down at Mariah curled softly in his arms, blood pulsed and gathered hotly, driven by the redoubled beating of his heart, blood surging with a relentless force that was tangible proof of his vulnerability to Mariah's sensual lures. Silently he cursed the fate that gave men hunger and women the instinctive cunning to use men's hunger against them.

"Put both hands on the rails," he said curtly.

When Mariah tried to respond to the clipped command, she found she couldn't move. Cash's arm was a steel band holding her against a body that also felt like steel. Discreetly she tried to put some distance between herself and the man whose eyes had the indigo violence of a stormy twilight. The quarter inch she gained by subtle squirming wasn't enough to allow her left hand to reach across her body to the corral fence. She tried for another quarter inch.

"What the hell do you think you're doing?" Cash snarled.

"I'm trying to follow your orders."

"When did I order you to rub against me like a cat in heat?"

Shock, disbelief and indignation showed on Mariah's face, followed by anger. She shoved hard against his chest. "Let go of me!"

She might as well have tried to push away the mountain itself. All her struggles accomplished were further small movements that had the effect of teaching her how powerful and hard Cash's body was—and how soft her own was by comparison. The lesson should have frightened her. Instead, it sent warmth stealing through her, gentle pulses of heat that came from the secret places of her body. The sensations were as exquisite as they were unexpected.

"C-Cash . . . ?"

The catch in Mariah's voice sent a lightning stroke of desire arcing through Cash. For an instant his arm tightened even more, pinning Mariah to the hungry length of his body. Then he spun her around to face the corral, clamped her left hand over the top rail of the corral and let go of her. When her knees sagged, he caught her around the ribs with both hands, taking care to hold her well away from his body. Unfortunately there was nothing he could do about her breasts curving so close to his fingers, her soft flesh moving in searing caress each time she took a breath.

"Stand up, damn it," Cash said through clenched teeth, "or I swear I'll let you fall."

Mariah took in a shuddering breath, wondering if the jolting ride to Black Springs had scrambled her brains as well as her legs. The weakness melting her bones right now owed nothing to the hours on horseback and everything to the presence of the man whose heat reached out to her, surrounding her. She took another breath, then another, hanging on to the corral fence with what remained of her strength.

"I'm all right," Mariah said finally.

"Like hell. You're shaking."

"I'll survive."

With a muttered word, Cash let go of Mariah. His hands hovered close to her, ready to catch her if she fell. She didn't. She just sagged. Slowly she straightened.

"Now walk," he said.

"What?"

"You heard me. Walk."

A swift look over her shoulder told Mariah that Cash wasn't kidding. He expected her not only to stand on her rubbery legs but also to walk. Painfully she began inching crabwise along the corral fence, hanging on to the top rail with both hands. To her surprise, the exercise helped. Strength returned rapidly to her legs. Soon she was moving almost normally. She turned to give Cash a triumphant smile, only to discover that he was walking away. She started after him, decided it was a bit too soon to get beyond reach of the corral fence's support, and grabbed the sun-warmed wood again.

By the time Mariah felt confident enough to venture away from the fence, Cash had the horses taken care of and was carrying supplies into the line shack. The closer she walked to the slightly leaning building, the more she agreed that "shack" was the proper term. Tentatively she looked in the front—and only—door.

Cash hadn't been lying when he described the line shack's rudimentary comforts. Built for only occasional use by cowhands working a distant corner of the Rocking M's summer grazing range, the cabin consisted of four walls, a ceiling, a plank floor laid down over dirt, and two windows. The fireplace was rudely constructed of local rocks. The long tongue of soot that climbed the exterior stone above the hearth spoke eloquently of a chimney that didn't draw.

"I warned you," Cash said, brushing by Mariah.

"I didn't say a word."

"You didn't have to."

He dumped her backpack and makeshift bedroll on the floor near the fireplace. Puffs of dust arose.

"If you still want to go to Black Springs, put on your swimsuit," Cash said, turning away. "And wear shoes unless you want to ride there."

"Ride?" she asked weakly. "Uh, no thanks. How far is it?"

"I never measured it."

Mariah's small sigh was lost in the ghastly creaking the door made as it shut. She changed into her swimsuit as quickly as her protesting leg muscles allowed. The inexpensive tank suit was made of a thin, deep rose fabric that fit without clinging when it was dry. Wet, it was another matter. It would cling more closely than body heat. Since Mariah had been dry when she purchased the suit, she hadn't known about its split personality.

"Hey, tenderfoot. You ready yet?"

Groaning, Mariah finished tying her shoelaces and struggled to her feet. "I'm coming."

As she stood, she felt oddly undressed. If she had been barefoot in the bathing suit, she would have had no problem. But somehow wearing shoes made her feel . . . naked. She grabbed her windbreaker and put it on. The lightweight jacket was several sizes too big. Normally she wore it over a blouse and bulky sweater, so the extra room was appreciated. With only the thin tank suit to take up room, the windbreaker reached almost halfway down her thighs, giving her a comforting feeling of being adequately covered.

When Cash heard the front door creak, he turned around. His first impression was of long, elegant, naked legs. His second impression was the same. He felt a nearly overwhelming desire to unzip the jacket and see what was beneath. Anything, even the skimpiest string bikini, would

have been less arousing than the tantalizing impression of
nakedness lying just beneath the loose black windbreaker.

Mariah walked tentatively toward Cash, wondering at the
harsh expression on his face.

"Which way to the hot tub?" she asked, her voice deter-
minedly light.

Without a word Cash turned and walked around to the
back of the cabin. Mariah followed as quickly as she could,
picking her way along the clear stream that ran behind the
cabin. Even if her legs hadn't been shaky, she would have
had a hard time keeping up with Cash's long stride. When
her path took her on a hopscotch crossing of the creek, she
bent and tested the temperature of the water. It was icy.

"So much for my hot tub fantasy," she muttered.

The racing, glittering water came from a narrow gap in
the mountainside that was no more than fifty yards from the
cabin. Inside the gap the going became harder, a scramble
along a cascade that hissed and foamed with the force of its
downhill race. The rocks were dark, almost black, which
only added to the feeling of chill. Just when Mariah was
wondering if the effort would be worth it, she realized that
the mist peeling off the water was warm.

A hundred feet later the land leveled off to reveal a series
of graceful, stair-step pools that were rimmed by smooth
travertine and embroidered by satin waterfalls no more than
three feet high. As Mariah stared, a shiver of awe went over
her. The pools could not have been more beautiful if they
had been designed by an artist and built of golden marble.

The water in the lowest pool was a pale turquoise Mariah
had seen only on postcards of tropical islands. The water in
the next pool was a luminous aquamarine. The water in the
last pool shaded from turquoise to aquamarine to a clear,
very dark blue that was the exact shade of Cash's eyes. At
the far end of the highest pool, the water was so deep it appeared black but for swirls of shimmering indigo where liquid welled up from the depths of the earth in silent,

inexhaustible pulses that had begun long before man ever walked the western lands and would continue long after man left.

Slowly Mariah sank to her knees and extended her hand toward the jeweled beauty of the pool. Before she could touch the water, Cash snatched her hand back.

"I've cooked trout at this end of Black Springs. Sometimes the downstream end of the pool is cool enough to bear touching for a few moments. Most often it isn't. It depends."

"On what?"

Cash didn't answer her directly. "You get hot springs when groundwater sinks down until it reaches a body of magma and then flashes into superheated steam," he said, absently running his thumb over Mariah's palm as he looked at the slowly twisting depth of Black Springs. "The steam slams up through cracks in the country rock until the water bursts through to the surface of the land in a geyser or a hot spring. Most often the water never breaks the surface. It simply cools and sinks back down the cracks until it encounters magma, flashes to steam and surges upward again."

Mariah made a small sound, reflection of the sensations that were radiating up from her captive hand. Cash looked away from the water and realized that his thumb was caressing Mariah's palm in the rhythm of the water pulsing deep within the springs. With a muttered word, he released her hand.

"I can tell you how a hot spring works, but I can't tell you why some days Black Springs is too hot and other days it's bearable. So be careful every day. Even on its best behavior, Black Springs is dangerously hot a foot beneath the surface."

"Is the water drinkable?" she asked.

"Once it cools off the trout love it. So do I. It has a flavor better than wine."

Mariah stared wistfully at the beautiful, intensely clear, searingly hot water. "It looks so wonderful."

"Come on," Cash said, taking pity on her. "I'll show you the best place to soak out the aches." He led her back to the middle pool. "The closer you are to the spring, the hotter the water. Start at the lower end and work your way up until you're comfortable." He started to turn away, then stopped. "You *do* swim, don't you?"

Mariah glanced at the pool. "Sure, but that water is hardly deep enough for me to get wet sitting down."

"The pool is so clear it fools your eyes. At the far end, the water is over my head." Cash turned away. "If you're not back in an hour, I'll come back and drag you out. I'm hungry."

"You don't have to wait for me," she said, setting shoes and socks aside.

"The hell I don't. You're the cook, remember?"

Seven

On the fourth day, Mariah didn't have to be awakened by the sound of the front door creaking as Cash walked out to check on the horses. She woke up as soon as sunrise brightened the undraped windows. Silently she struggled out of her tangle of blankets. Although she still ached in odd places and she wished that she had brought a few more blankets to cushion the rough wood floor, she no longer woke up feeling as though she had been beaten and left out in the rain.

Shivering in the shack's chill air, Mariah knelt between her blankets and Cash's still-occupied sleeping bag as she worked over the ashes of last night's fire. As always, she had slept fully clothed, for the high mountain nights were cold even in summer. Yet as soon as the sun shone over the broken ramparts of Devil's Peak, the temperature rose swiftly, sometimes reaching the eighties by noon. So while Mariah slept wearing everything she had brought except her shoes, she shed layers throughout the morning, adding them again as the sun began its downward curve across the sky.

Enough coals remained in the hearth to make a handful of dry pine needles burst into flames after only a few instants. Mariah fed twigs into the fire, then bigger pieces, and finally stove-length wood. Despite the fireplace's sooty front, little smoke crept out into the room this morning. The chimney drew quite well so long as there wasn't a hard wind from the northeast.

When she was satisfied with the fire's progress, Mariah turned to the camp stove that she privately referred to as Beelzebub. It was the most perverse piece of machinery she had ever encountered. No matter how hard or how often she pumped up the pressure, the flame wobbled and sputtered and was barely hot enough to warm skin. When Cash pumped up the stove, however, it put out a flame that could cut through steel.

With a muttered prayer, Mariah reached for the camp stove. A tanned, rather hairy hand shot out of Cash's sleeping bag and wrapped around her wrist, preventing her from touching the stove.

"I'll take care of it."

"Thanks. The thing hates me."

There was muffled laughter as a flap of the partially zipped sleeping bag was shoved aside, revealing Cash's head and bare shoulders. Another big hand closed over Mariah's. He rubbed her hand lightly between his own warm palms. Long, strong, randomly scarred fingers moved almost caressingly over her skin. She shivered, but it had nothing to do with the temperature in the cabin.

"You really *are* cold," he said in a deep voice.

"You're not. You're like fire."

"No, I mean it," Cash said. He propped himself up on one elbow and pulled Mariah's hands toward himself. "Your fingers are like ice. No wonder you thrash around half the night. Why didn't you tell me you were cold?"

"Sorry." Mariah tugged discreetly at her hands. They remained captive to Cash's enticing warmth. "I didn't mean to keep you awake."

"To hell with that. Why didn't you tell me?"

"I was afraid you'd use it as an excuse to make me go back."

Cash hissed a single harsh word and sat up straight. The sleeping bag slithered down his torso. If he was wearing anything besides the bag, it didn't show. Although Mariah had seen Cash at Black Springs dressed in only cutoff jeans, somehow it just wasn't the same as seeing him rising half-naked from the warm folds of a sleeping bag. A curling, masculine pelt went in a ragged wedge from Cash's collarbones to a hand span above his navel. Below the navel a dark line no thicker than her finger descended into the undiscovered territory concealed by the sleeping bag.

"It's not worth getting upset about," Mariah said quickly, looking away. "Any extra calories I burn at night I replace at breakfast, and then some. Speaking of which, do you want pancakes again? Or do you want biscuits and bacon? Or do you just want to grab some trail mix and go prospecting? I'm going with you today. I'm not stiff anymore. I won't be a drag on you. I promise."

There was a long silence while Cash looked at Mariah and she looked at the fire that was struggling to burn cold wood. Deliberately he cupped her hands in his own, brought them to his mouth, and blew warm air over her chilled skin. Before she had recovered from the shock of feeling his lips brushing over her palms, he was rubbing her hands against his chest, holding her between his palms and the heat of his big body. It was like being toasted between two fires.

"Better?" he asked quietly after a minute.

Mariah nodded, afraid to trust her voice.

With a squeeze so gentle that she might have imagined it, Cash released her hands and began dressing. For a few moments Mariah couldn't move. When she went to measure ingredients for biscuits, her hands were warm, but trembling. She was glad Cash was too busy dressing to notice.

The front door creaked as he went outside. A few minutes later it creaked again when he returned. The smell of dew and evergreen resin came back inside with him.

"If that's biscuits and bacon, make a double batch," Cash said. "We'll eat them on the trail for lunch."

"Sure." Then the meaning of his words penetrated. Mariah turned toward him eagerly. "Does that mean I get to come along?"

"That's what you're here for, isn't it?" Cash asked curtly, but he was smiling.

She grinned and turned back to the fire, carefully positioning the reflector oven. She had discovered the oven in a corner of the shack along with other cooking supplies Cash rarely ever used. Her first few attempts to cook with the oven had been a disaster, but there had been little else for her to do except experiment with camp cooking while Cash was off exploring and she was recovering from the ride to Devil's Peak.

Mariah had been grateful to be able to keep the disasters a secret and pretend that the successes were commonplace. It had been worth all the frustration and singed fingertips to see Cash's expression when he walked into the line shack after a day of prospecting and found fresh biscuits, fried ham, baked beans with molasses and a side dish of fresh watercress and tender young dandelion greens waiting for him.

While the coffee finished perking on the stove and the last batch of bacon sizzled fragrantly in the frying pan, Mariah sliced two apples and piled a mound of bacon on a tin plate. She surrounded the crisp bacon with biscuits and set the plate on the floor near the fireplace, where a squeeze bottle of honey was slowly warming. She poured two cups of coffee and settled cross-legged on the floor in front of the food.

The position caused only a twinge or two in her thigh muscles.

"Come and get it," Mariah called out.

Cash looked up from the firewood he had been stacking in a corner of the shack. For a moment he was motionless, trying to decide which looked more tempting—the food or the lithe young woman who had proven to be such good company. Too good. It would have been much easier on him if she had been sulky or petulant or even indifferent—anything but humorous and quick and so aware of him as a man that her hands shook when he touched her.

The tactile memory of Mariah's cool, trembling fingers still burned against his chest. It had taken all of his self-control not to pull her soft hands down into the sleeping bag and let her discover just how hot he really was.

Damn you, Luke. Why didn't you tell me to leave your sister alone? Why did you give me a green flag when you know me well enough to know I don't have marriage in mind? And why can't I look at Mariah without getting hot?

There was no answer to Cash's furious thoughts. There was only fragrance and steamy heat as he pulled apart a biscuit, and then a rush of pleasure as he savored the flavor and tenderness of the food Mariah had prepared for him.

They ate in a silence that was punctuated by the small sounds of silverware clicking against metal plates, the muted whisper of the fire and the almost secretive rustle of clothes as one or the other of them reached for the honey. When Cash could eat no more, he took a sip of coffee, sighed, and looked at Mariah.

"Thanks," he said.

"For what?"

"Being a good cook."

She laughed, but her pleasure in the compliment was as clear as the golden glow of her eyes. "It's the least I could do. I know you didn't want me to come with you."

"And you're used to being not wanted, aren't you." There was no question in Cash's voice, simply the certainty that had come of watching her in the past days.

Mariah hesitated, then shrugged. "Harold—my mother's second husband—didn't like me. Nothing I did in fifteen years changed that. I spent most of those years at girls' boarding schools and summer camps." She smiled crookedly. "That's where I learned to ride, hike, make camp fires, put up a tent, cook, sew, give first aid, braid thin plastic thongs into thick useless cords, make unspeakably ugly things in clay, and identify poisonous snakes and spiders."

"A well-rounded education," Cash said, hiding a grin.

Mariah laughed. "You know, it really was. A lot of girls never get a chance at all to be outdoors. Some of the girls hated it, of course. Most just took it in stride. I loved it. The trees and rocks and critters didn't care that your real father never wrote to you, that your stepfather couldn't stand to be in the same room with you, or that your mother's grip on reality was as fragile as a summer frost."

Cash drained his coffee cup, then said simply, "Luke wrote to you."

"What?"

"Luke has written to you at least twice a year for as long as I've known him," Cash said as he poured himself more coffee. "Christmas and your birthday. He sent gifts, too. Nothing ever came back. Not a single word."

"I didn't know. I never saw them. But I wrote to him. Mother mailed..." Realization came, darkening Mariah's eyes. "She never mailed my letters. She never let me see Luke's."

The strained quality of Mariah's voice made Cash glance up sharply. Reflected firelight glittered in the tears running down her cheeks. He set aside his coffee and reached for her, brushing tears away with the back of his fingers.

"Hey, I didn't mean to hurt you," Cash said, stroking her cheek with a gentleness surprising in such a big man.

"I know," Mariah whispered. "It's just . . . I used to lie awake and cry on Christmas and my birthday because I was alone. But I wasn't alone, not really, and I didn't even know it." She closed her eyes and laced her fingers tightly together to keep from reaching for Cash, from crawling into his lap and asking to be held. "Poor Luke," she whispered. "He must have felt so lonely, too." She hesitated, then asked in a rush, "Your sister loves Luke, doesn't she? Truly loves him?"

"Carla has always loved Luke."

Mariah heard the absolute certainty in Cash's voice and let out a long sigh. "Thank God. Luke deserves to be loved. He's a good man."

Cash looked down at Mariah's face. Her eyes were closed. Long, dark eyelashes were tipped with diamond tears. All that kept him from bending down and sipping teardrops from her lashes was the certainty that anything he began wouldn't end short of his becoming her lover. Her sadness had made her too vulnerable right now—and it made him too vulnerable, as well. The urge to comfort her in the most elemental way of all was almost overwhelming. He wanted her far too much to trust his self-control.

"Yes," Cash said as he stood up in a controlled rush of power. "Luke is a good man." He jammed his hands into his back jeans pockets to keep from reaching for Mariah. "If we're going to get any prospecting done, we'd better get going. From the looks of the sky, we'll have a thunderstorm by afternoon."

"The dishes will take only a minute," Mariah said, blotting surreptitiously at her cheeks with her shirttail.

It was longer than a minute, but Cash made no comment when Mariah emerged from the cabin wearing her backpack. He put his hand underneath her pack, hefted it, and calmly peeled it from her shoulders.

"I can carry it," Mariah said quickly.

Cash didn't even bother to reply. He simply transferred the contents of her backpack to his own, put it on and asked, "Ever panned for gold?"

She shook her head.

"It's harder than it looks," he said.

"Isn't everything?"

Cash smiled crookedly. "Yeah, I guess it is." He looked at Mariah's soft shoes, frowned and looked away. "I'm going to try a new area of the watershed. It could get rough, so I want you to promise me something."

Warily Mariah looked up. "What?"

"When you need help—and you will—let me know. I don't want to pack you out of here with a broken ankle."

"I'll ask for help. But it would be nice," she added wistfully, "if you wouldn't bite my head off when I ask."

Cash grunted. "Since you've never panned for gold and we're in a hurry, I'll do the panning. If you really want to learn, I'll teach you later. Come on. Time's a-wasting."

The pace Cash set was hard but not punishing. Mariah didn't complain. She was certain the pace would have been even faster if Cash had been alone.

There was no trail to follow. From time to time Cash consulted a compass, made cryptic notes in a frayed notebook, and then set off over the rugged land once more, usually in a different direction. Mariah watched the landscape carefully, orienting herself from various landmarks each time Cash changed direction. After half an hour they reached a stream that was less than six feet wide. It rushed over and around pale granite boulders in a silver-white blur that shaded into brilliant turquoise where the water slowed and deepened.

Cash shrugged out of his backpack and untied a broad, flat pan, which looked rather like a shallow wok. Pan in one hand, short-handled shovel in the other, he sat on his heels by the stream. With a deft motion he scooped out a shovel full of gravel from the eddy of water behind a boulder. He dumped the shovel-load into the gold pan, shook it, and picked over the contents. Bigger pieces of quartz and granite were discarded without hesitation, despite the fact that some of them had a golden kind of glitter that made Mariah's heart beat faster and her breath catch audibly.

"Mica," Cash explained succinctly, dumping another handful of rocks back in the stream.

"Oh." Mariah sighed. Her reading on the subject of granite, gold, and prospecting had told her about mica. It was pretty, but it was as common as sand.

"All that glitters isn't gold, remember?" he asked, giving her an amused, sideways glance.

She grimaced.

Cash laughed and scooped up enough water to begin washing the material remaining in the bottom of the gold pan. A deft motion of his wrists sent the water swirling around in a neat circle. When he tilted the pan slightly away from himself, the circular movement of the water lifted the lighter particles away from the bottom of the pan. Water and particles climbed the shallow incline to the rim and drained back into the stream. After a minute or two, Cash looked at the remaining stuff, rubbed it between his fingers, stared again, and flipped it all back into the stream. He rinsed the pan, attached it and the shovel to his backpack again, and set off upstream.

"Nothing, huh?" Mariah said, scrambling to keep up.

"Grit, sand, pea gravel, pebbles. Granite. Some basalt. A bit of chert. Small piece of clear quartz."

"No gold?"

"Not even pyrite. That's fool's gold."

"I know. Pyrite is pretty, though."

Cash grunted. "Leave it to a woman to think pretty is enough."

"Oh, right. That's why men have such a marked preference for ugly women."

Cash hid a smile. For a time there was silence punctuated by scrambling sounds when the going became especially slippery at the stream's edge. Twice Mariah needed help. The first time she needed only a steadying hand as she scrambled forward. The second time Cash found it easier simply to lift her over the obstacle. The feel of his hands on her, and the ease with which he moved her from place to place, left Mariah more than a little breathless. Yet despite the odd fluttering in the pit of her stomach, her brain continued to work.

"Cash?"

The sound he made was encouraging rather than curt, so Mariah continued.

"What are we doing?"

"Walking upstream."

"Why are we walking upstream?"

"It's called prospecting, honey. Long hours, backbreaking work and no pay. Just like I told you back at the ranch house. Remember?"

Mariah sighed and tried another approach.

"We're looking for Mad Jack's mine, right?" she asked.

"Right."

"Mad Jack's gold was rough, which meant it didn't come out of a placer pocket in a stream, right?"

"Right."

"Because placer gold is smooth."

"Right."

The amusement in Cash's tone was almost tangible. It was also gentle rather than disdainful. Knowing that she was being teased, yet beguiled by the method, Mariah persisted.

"Then why are you panning for Mad Jack's nonplacer mine?"

Cash's soft laughter barely rose above the sound of the churning stream. He turned around, made a lightning grab and had Mariah securely tucked against his chest before she knew what was happening. With a startled sound she hung on to him as he crossed the stream in a few strides, his boots impervious to the cold water.

"Wondered when you'd catch on," Cash said.

He set Mariah back on her feet, releasing her with a slow reluctance that was like a caress. His smile was the same. A caress.

"But the truth is," he continued in a deep voice, resolutely looking away from her, "I *am* panning for that mine. Think about it. Gold is heavy. Wherever a gold-bearing formation breaks the surface, gradually the matrix surrounding the gold weathers away. Gold doesn't weather. That, and its malleability, is what makes it so valuable to man."

Mariah made an encouraging sound.

"Anyway, the matrix crumbles away and frees the gold, which is heavy for its size. Gravity takes hold, pulling the gold downhill until it reaches a stream and sinks to the bottom. Floods scoop out the gold and beat it around and drop it off farther downstream. Slowly the gold migrates downhill, getting more and more round until the nugget settles down to bedrock in a deep placer pocket."

"Mad Jack's gold is rough," Mariah pointed out.

"Yeah. I'm betting that canny old bastard panned a nameless stream and found bits of gold that were so rough they had to have come from a place nearby. So he panned that watershed, tracking the color to its source—the mother lode."

Cash looked back at Mariah to see if she understood. What he saw were wisps of dark, shiny hair feathered across her face, silky strands lifted by a cool wind. Before he could stop himself, he smoothed the hair away from her lips and wide golden eyes. Her pupils dilated as her breath came in fast and hard.

"You see," he said, his voice husky, "streams are a prospector's best friend. They collect and concentrate gold.

Without them a lot of the West's most famous gold strikes would never have been made.''

''Really?''

The breathless quality of Mariah's voice was a caress that shivered delicately over Cash.

''They're still looking for the mother lode that put Sutter's Mill on the map,'' he murmured, catching a lock of her hair and running it between his fingers.

The soft sound Mariah made could have been a response to his words or to the fragile brush of Cash's fingertips at her hairline. With a stifled curse at his inability to keep his hands off her, Cash opened his fingers, releasing Mariah from silken captivity.

''Anyway,'' he said, turning his attention back to the rugged countryside, ''I'm betting Mad Jack was panning a granite-bottomed stream, because only a fool looks for gold in lava formations, and that old boy was nobody's fool.''

''You're not a fool, either,'' Mariah said huskily, grabbing desperately for a safe topic, because it was that or grab Cash's hand and beg him to go on touching her. ''So why were you prospecting the Devil's Peak area before you saw Mad Jack's map? Until we got to this stream, I didn't see anything that looked like granite or quartzite or any of the 'ites' that are usually found with gold. Just all kinds of lava. Granted, I'm no expert on gold hunting, but . . .''

''This area wasn't my first choice,'' Cash said dryly. ''Almost two years ago I was having a soak in Black Springs when I realized that Devil's Peak is basically a volcano rammed through and poured out over country rock that's largely granite. Where the lava has eroded enough, the granite shows through. And where there's granite, there could be gold.'' He smiled, gave Mariah a sideways glance, and admitted, ''I was glad to see that ratty old map, though. I've been panning up here for two years and haven't gotten anything more to show for it than a tired back.''

''No gold at all?''

"A bit of color here and there. Hobbyist flakes, the kind you put in a magnifying vial and show to patient friends. Nothing to raise the blood pressure."

"Darn, I was hoping that—trout!" Mariah said excitedly, pointing toward the stream.

"What?"

"I just saw a trout! Look!"

Smiling down at Mariah, barely resisting the urge to fold her against his body in a long hug, Cash didn't even glance at the stream that had captured her interest.

"Fish are silver," he said in a deep voice. "We're after gold. We'll catch dinner on the way back."

"How can you be so sure? The fish could be hiding under rocks by then."

"They won't be."

Mariah made an unconvinced sound.

"I bet we'll catch our fill of trout for dinner tonight," Cash said.

"What do you bet?"

"Loser cleans the fish."

"What if there are no fish to clean?"

"There will be."

"You're on," she retorted quickly, forgetting Nevada's advice about never gambling with a man called Cash. "If we don't get fish, you do dishes tonight."

"Yeah?"

"Yeah."

"You're on, lady." Cash laughed softly and tugged at a silky lock of Mariah's hair once more. "Candy from a baby."

"Tell me that while you're doing dishes."

Cash just laughed.

"It's not a bet until we shake on it," she said, holding out her hand.

"That's not how it works between a man and a woman."

He took her hand and brought it to his mouth. She felt the mild rasp of his growing beard, the brush of his lips over her palm, and a single hot touch from the tip of his tongue. She thought Cash whispered *candy* when he straightened, but she was too shaken to be sure.

"Now it's a bet," he said.

Eight

"How's it going?" Cash asked.

Mariah looked up from the last fish that remained to be cleaned. "Better for me than for the trout."

He laughed and watched as she prepared the fish for the frying pan with inexpert but nonetheless effective swipes of his filleting knife.

Cash had expected Mariah to balk at paying off the bet, or at the very least to sulk over it. Instead, she had attacked the fish with the same lack of complaint she had shown for sleeping on the shack's cold, drafty floor. Only her unconscious sigh of relief as she rinsed the last fish—and her hands—in the icy stream told Cash how little she had liked the chore.

"I'll do the dishes," he said as she finished.

"Not a chance. It's the only way I'll get the smell of fish off my hands."

Cash grabbed one of Mariah's hands, held it under his nose and inhaled dramatically. "Smells fine to me."

"You must be hungry."

"How did you guess?"

"You're alive," she said, laughing up at him.

Smiling widely, Cash grabbed the tin plate of fish in one hand. The other still held Mariah's water-chilled fingers. He pulled her to her feet with ease.

"Lady, you have the coldest hands of any woman I've ever known."

"Try me after I've done the dishes," she retorted.

He smiled down at her. "Okay."

Mariah's stomach gave a tiny little flip that became a definite flutter when Cash pulled her fingers up his body and tucked them against the warm curve of his neck. Whether it was his body heat or the increased beating of her own heart, Mariah's fingers warmed up very quickly. She slanted brief, sideways glances at Cash as they walked toward the line shack, but he apparently felt that warming her cold hands on his body was in the same category as helping her over rough spots in the trail—no big deal. Certainly it wasn't something for him to go all breathless over.

But Mariah was. Breathless. Each time Cash touched her she felt strange, almost shaky, yet the sensations shimmering through her body were very sweet. Even as she wondered if Cash felt the same, she discarded the idea. He was so matter-of-fact about any physical contact that it made her response to it look foolish.

"Listen," Cash said, stopping suddenly.

Mariah froze. From the direction of Devil's Peak came a low, fluid, rushing sound, as though there were a river racing by just out of sight. Yet she knew there wasn't.

"What is it?" she whispered.

"Wind. See? It's bending the evergreens on the slope like an invisible hand stroking fur. The rain is about a quarter mile behind."

Mariah followed the direction of his pointing finger and saw that Cash was right. Heralded by a fierce, transparent cataract of wind, a storm was sweeping rapidly toward them across the slope of Devil's Peak.

"Unless you want the coldest shower you ever took," Cash said, "stretch those long legs."

A crack of thunder underlined Cash's words. He grabbed the plate of fish from Mariah and pushed her in the direction of the cabin.

"Run for it!"

"What about you?"

"Move, lady!"

Mariah bolted for the cabin, still feeling the imprint of Cash's hand on her bottom, where he had emphasized his command with a definite smack. She barely beat the speeding storm back to the line shack's uncertain shelter.

Cash, who had the plate of slippery fish to balance, couldn't move as quickly as Mariah. The difference in reaching shelter was only a minute or two, but it was enough. He got soaked. Swearing at the icy rain, Cash bolted through the line shack's open door and kicked it shut behind him. Water ran off his big body and puddled around his feet.

"Put all the stuff that has to stay dry over there," Cash said loudly, trying to be heard over the hammering of rain on the roof.

Mariah grabbed bedding, clothes and dry food and started stacking them haphazardly in the corner Cash had indicated. He set aside the fish and disappeared outside again. Moments later he returned, his arms piled high with firewood. The wood dripped as much as he did, adding to the puddles that were appearing magically on the floor in every area of the cabin but one—the corner where Mariah was frantically storing things. Cash dumped the firewood near the hearth and went back outside again. Almost instantly he reappeared, arms loaded with wood once more. With swift, efficient motions he began stacking the wood according to size.

"Don't forget the kindling," he said without looking up.

Quickly Mariah rescued a burlap sack of dry pine needles and kindling from the long tongue of water that was creeping across the floor. Before the puddle could reach the dry corner, gaps in the wooden planks of the floor drained the water away.

"At least it leaks on the bottom, too," Mariah said.

"Damn good thing. Otherwise we'd drown."

Thunder cracked and rolled down from the peak in an avalanche of sound.

"What about the horses?" Mariah asked.

"They'll get wet just like they would at the home corral."

Cash stood up and shook his head, spraying cold drops everywhere.

"We had a dog that used to do that," Mariah said. "We kept him outside when it rained. In Seattle, that was most of the time."

She started to say something else, then forgot what it was. Cash was peeling off his flannel shirt and arranging it on a series of nails over the hearth. The naked reality of his strength fascinated her. Every twist of his body, every motion, every breath, shifted the masculine pattern of bone and muscle, sinew and tendon, making new arrangements of light and shadow, strength and grace.

"Is something wrong?" Cash said, both amused and aroused by the admiration in Mariah's golden eyes.

"Er... you're steaming."

"What?"

"You're steaming."

Cash held out his arms and laughed as he saw that Mariah was right. Heat curled visibly up from his body in the line shack's chilly air.

"I'll get you a shirt before you freeze," Mariah said, turning back to the haphazard mound she had piled in the corner. She rummaged about until she came up with a midnight-blue shirt that was the color of Cash's eyes in the stormy light. "I knew it was here."

"Thanks. Can you find some jeans, too?"

The voice came from so close to Mariah that she was startled. She glanced around and saw bare feet not eight inches away. Bare calves, too. And knees. And thighs. And—hastily she looked back at the pile of dry goods, hoping Cash couldn't see the sudden color burning on her cheeks or the clumsiness of her hands.

But Cash saw both the heat in Mariah's cheeks and the trembling of her fingers as she handed him dry jeans without looking around.

"Sorry," he said, taking the jeans from her and stepping into them. "In these days of co-ed dorms, I didn't think the sight of a man in underwear would embarrass you."

"There's rather a lot of you," Mariah said in an elaborately casual voice, then put her face in her hands. "I didn't mean it the way it sounded. It's just that you're bigger than most men and ... and ..."

"Taller, too," Cash said blandly.

Mariah made a muffled sound behind her hands, and then another.

"You're laughing at me," he said.

"No, I'm strangling on my feet."

"Try putting them in your mouth only one at a time. It always works for me."

Mariah gave up and laughed out loud. Smiling, Cash listened to her laughter glittering through the drumroll of rain on the roof. He was still smiling when he went down on one knee in front of the fire and stirred it into life.

"What do you say to an early dinner and a game of cards?" Cash asked.

"Sure. What kind of game?"

"Poker. Is there any other kind?"

"Zillions. Canasta and gin and Fish and Old Maid and—"

"Kid games," Cash interrupted, scoffing. He looked over his shoulder and saw Mariah watching him. "We're too old for that."

The gleaming intensity of Cash's eyes made Mariah feel weak.

"I just remembered something," she said faintly.

"What?"

"Never play cards with a man called Cash."

"It doesn't apply. My name is Alexander."

"I'm reassured."

"Thought you would be."

"I'm also broke."

"That's okay. We'll play for things we have lots of."

"Like what?"

"Pine needles, smiles, puddles, kisses, raindrops, that sort of thing." Without waiting for an answer, Cash turned back to the fire. "How hot do you need it for trout? Or do you want to cook them over the camp stove?"

Blinking, Mariah tried to gather her scattered thoughts. Cash couldn't have mentioned kisses, could he? She must have been letting her own longing guide her hearing down false trails.

"Trout," she said tentatively.

"Yeah. You remember. Those slippery little devils you cleaned." He smiled. "The look on your face... Never bet anything you mind losing, honey."

Abruptly Mariah was certain she had heard his list of betting items very clearly, and kisses had definitely been one of them.

And he had nearly gotten away with it.

"Cash McQueen, you could teach slippery to a fish."

He laughed out loud, enjoying Mariah's quick tongue. Then he thought of some other ways he would like to enjoy that tongue. The fit of his jeans changed abruptly. So did his laughter. He stood in a barely controlled rush of power and turned his back on Mariah.

"You'll need light to cook," he muttered.

He crossed the shack in a few long strides, ignoring the puddles, and yanked a pressurized gas lantern from its wall hook. He pumped up the lantern with short, savage strokes, ripped a wooden match into life on his jeans and lit the lantern. Light pulsed wildly, erratically, until he adjusted the gas feed. The lantern settled into a hard, bright light whose pulses were so subtle they were almost undetectable. He brought the lantern across the room and hung it on one of the many nails that cowhands had driven into the line shack's walls over the years.

"Thank you," Mariah said uncertainly, wondering if Cash had somehow been insulted by being called slippery. But his laughter had been genuine. Then he had stopped laughing and that, too, had been genuine.

With a muffled sigh Mariah concentrated on preparing dinner. While she worked, Cash prowled the six-foot-by-nine-foot shack, putting pans and cups and other containers under the worst leaks. Rain hammered down with the single-minded ferocity of a high-country storm. Although it was hours from sunset, the light level dropped dramatically. Except for occasional violent flashes of lightning, the hearth and lantern became isolated islands of illumination in the gloom.

Both Cash and Mariah ate quickly, for the metal camp plates drained heat from the food. Cash stripped the sweet flesh from the fish bones with a deftness that spoke of long practice. Cornbread steamed and breathed fragrance into the chilly air. When there was nothing left but crumbs and memories, Mariah reached for the dishes.

"I'll do them," Cash said. "You've had a hard day."

"No worse than yours."

Cash didn't argue, he simply shaved soap into a pot with his lethally sharp pocketknife, added water that had been warming in the bucket by the hearth and began washing dishes. Mariah rinsed and stacked the dishes to one side to drain, watching him from the corner of her eyes. He had rolled up his sleeves to deal with the dishes. Each movement he made revealed the muscular power of his forearms and the blunt strength in his hands.

When the dishes were over and Cash sat cross-legged opposite Mariah on the only dry patch of floor in the cabin, lantern light poured over him, highlighting the planes of his face, the sensual lines of his mouth, and the sheer power of his body. As Cash quickly dealt the cards, Mariah watched him with a fascination she slowly stopped trying to hide.

The cards she picked up time after time received very little of her attention. As a result, the pile of dried pine needles in front of her vanished as though in an invisible fire. She didn't mind. She was too busy enjoying sitting with Cash in a cabin surrounded on the outside by storm and filled on the inside by the hushed silence of pent breath.

"Are puddles worth more than pine needles?" Mariah asked, looking at the three needles left to her.

"Only if you're thirsty."

"Are you?"

"I've got all the water I can stand right now."

Mariah smiled. "Yeah, I know what you mean. Well, that lets out raindrops, too. I guess I have to fold. I'm busted."

Cash nudged a palm-size pile of needles from his pile over to her side of the "table."

"What's that for?" she asked.

"Your smile."

"Really? All these needles? If that's what a smile is worth, how much for a kiss?"

Abruptly Cash looked up from his cards. His glance moved almost tangibly over Mariah's face, lingering with frank intensity on the curving line of her lips. Then he looked back at his cards, his expression bleak.

"More than either of us has," he said flatly.

Several hands were played in silence but for the hissing of the lantern and the slowly diminishing rush of rain. Cash kept winning, which meant that he kept dealing cards. As he did, the lantern picked out various small scars on his hands.

"How did you get these?" Mariah asked, touching the back of Cash's right hand with her fingertips.

He froze for an instant, then let out his breath so softly she didn't hear. Her fingers were cool, but they burned on his skin, making him burn, as well.

"You pan gold for more than a few minutes in these streams and your hands get numb," Cash said. His voice was unusually deep, almost hoarse, reflecting the quickening of his body. "I've cut myself and never even known it. Same for using the rock hammer during cold weather. Easiest thing in the world to zing yourself. What my own clumsiness doesn't cause, flying chips of rock take care of."

"Clumsy?" Mariah laughed. "If you're clumsy, I'm a trout."

"Then you're in trouble, honey. I'm still hungry."

"I'm a very, very *young* trout."

Cash smiled grimly. "Yeah. I keep reminding myself of that. You're what...twenty-two?"

Startled by the unexpected question, Mariah nodded.

"I teach grad students who are older than you," Cash said, his tone disgusted.

"So?"

"So quit looking at me with those big golden eyes and wondering what it would be like to kiss me."

Mariah's first impulse was to deny any such thoughts. Her second was the same. Her third was embarrassment that she was so transparent.

"You see," Cash said flatly, pinning Mariah with a look, "I'm wondering the same thing about you. But I'm not a college kid. If I start kissing you, I'm going to want more than a little taste of all that honey. I'm going to want everything you have to give a man, and I'm going to want it until I'm too damn tired to lick my lips. I get hard just watching you breathe, so teasing me into kissing you would be a really dumb idea, unless you're ready to quit playing and start screwing around.'' He watched Mariah's face, muttered something harsh under his breath, and threw a big handful of pine needles into the pot. ''Call and raise you.''

''I d-don't have that many needles.''

''Then you lose, don't you?'' he asked. And he waited.

How much is a kiss worth?

Mariah didn't speak the words aloud. She didn't have to. She knew without asking that a kiss would be worth every needle in the whole forest. In electric silence she looked at Cash's mouth with a hunger she had never felt before. The days of beard stubble enhanced rather than detracted from the smooth masculine invitation of his lips. And he was watching her with eyes that burned. He had meant his warning. If she teased him into kissing her, she had better be prepared for a lot more than a kiss.

The thought both shocked and fascinated Mariah. She had never wanted a man before. She wanted Cash now. She wanted to be kissed by him, to feel his arms around her, to feel his strength beneath her hands. But she had never been a man's lover before. She wasn't sure she was ready tonight, and Cash had made it very clear that there would be no way for her to test the water without getting in over her head.

''I guess I lose,'' Mariah whispered. ''But it isn't fair.''

''What isn't?''

''Not even one kiss, when you must have kissed a hundred other women.''

''Don't bet on it. I'm very particular about who gets close to me.'' Abruptly Cash closed his eyes against the yearning, tentative flames of desire in Mariah's golden glance. ''The game is over, Mariah. Go to bed. Now.''

Without a word Mariah abandoned her cards, rushed to her feet and began arranging her blankets for the night. After only a few moments she was ready for bed. She kicked out of her shoes, crawled into the cold nest she had made

IT'S FUN! IT'S FREE!
AND IT COULD MAKE YOU A
MILLIONAIRE

If you've ever played scratch-off lottery tickets, you should be familiar with how our games work. On each of the first four tickets (numbered 1 to 4 in the upper right) there are Pink Metallic Strips to scratch off.

Using a coin, do just that—carefully scratch the PINK strips to reveal how much each ticket could be worth if it is a winning ticket. Tickets could be worth from $10.00 to $1,000,000.00 in lifetime money.

Note, also, that each of your 4 tickets has a unique sweepstakes Lucky Number…and that's 4 chances for a **BIG WIN!**

FREE BOOKS!

At the same time you play your tickets for big prizes, you are invited to play ticket #5 for the chance to get one or more free book(s) from Silhouette. We give away free book(s) to introduce readers to the benefits of the Silhouette Reader Service™.

Accepting the free book(s) places you under no obligation to buy anything! You may keep your free book(s) and return the accompanying statement marked "cancel." But if we don't hear from you, then every month we'll deliver 6 of the newest Silhouette Desire® novels right to your door. You'll pay the low members-only price of just $2.24* each—a savings of 26¢ apiece off the cover price —plus 69¢ delivery per shipment! You may cancel at any time.

Of course, you may play "THE BIG WIN" without requesting any free book(s) by scratching tickets #1 through #4 only. But remember, that first shipment of one or more books is FREE!

PLUS A FREE GIFT!

One more thing, when you accept the free book(s) on ticket #5 you are also entitled to play ticket #6, which is GOOD FOR A GREAT GIFT! Like the book(s), this gift is totally free and yours to keep as thanks for giving our Reader Service a try!

So scratch off the PINK STRIPS on all your BIG WIN tickets and send for everything today! You've got nothing to lose and everything to gain!

Here are your BIG WIN Game Tickets, worth from $10.00 to $1,000,000.00 each. Scratch off the PINK METALLIC STRIP on each of your Sweepstakes tickets to see what you could win and mail your entry right away. (SEE OFFICIAL RULES IN BACK OF BOOK FOR DETAILS!)

This could be your lucky day - GOOD LUCK!

TICKET 1
Scratch PINK METALLIC STRIP to reveal potential value of this ticket if it is a winning ticket. Return all game tickets intact.

LUCKY NUMBER

1Q 178336

TICKET 2
Scratch PINK METALLIC STRIP to reveal potential value of this ticket if it is a winning ticket. Return all game tickets intact.

LUCKY NUMBER

3A 175179

TICKET 3
Scratch PINK METALLIC STRIP to reveal potential value of this ticket if it is a winning ticket. Return all game tickets intact.

LUCKY NUMBER

9W 186530

TICKET 4
Scratch PINK METALLIC STRIP to reveal potential value of this ticket if it is a winning ticket. Return all game tickets intact.

LUCKY NUMBER

5V 177317

TICKET 5
We're giving away brand new books to selected individuals. Scratch PINK METALLIC STRIP for number of free books you will receive.

AUTHORIZATION CODE

130107-742

TICKET 6
We have an outstanding added gift for you if you are accepting our free books. Scratch PINK METALLIC STRIP to reveal gift.

AUTHORIZATION CODE

130107-742

YES! Enter my Lucky Numbers in THE BIG WIN Sweepstakes and when winners are selected, tell me if I've won any prize. If PINK METALLIC STRIP is scratched off on ticket #5, I will also receive one or more FREE Silhouette Desire® novels along with the FREE GIFT on ticket #6, as explained on the opposite page.

(C-SIL-D-03/91) 326 CIS ACG2

NAME _____

ADDRESS _____ APT. _____

CITY _____ PROVINCE _____ POSTAL CODE _____

Carefully
detach card
along dotted
lines and
mail today!

Play
all your
BIG WIN
tickets
and get
everything
you're
entitled to-
including
FREE BOOKS
and a
FREE GIFT!

**Business
Reply Mail**

No Postage Stamp
Necessary if Mailed
in Canada

Postage will be paid by

**SILHOUETTE READER SERVICE
THE BIG WIN SWEEPSTAKES**

P.O. Box 609
Fort Erie, Ontario
L2A 9Z9

Canada Post
Postes Canada
125

and began shivering. The first few minutes in bed at night, and the first few out of it in the morning, were the coldest parts of the day.

Cash stood up and moved around the cabin, listening to the rain. When he had checked all the pans he turned off the lantern and knelt to bank the fire. Although Mariah tried not to watch him, it was impossible. Firelight turned his hair to molten gold and caressed his face the way she wanted to. Closing her eyes, shivering, she gripped the blankets even more tightly, taking what warmth she could from them.

"Here."

Mariah's eyes snapped open. Cash was looming above her. His hands moved as he unfurled a piece of cloth and pulled it over her. One side of the cloth was a metallic silver. The other was black.

"What is it?"

"Something developed by NASA," Cash said. He knelt next to Mariah and began tucking the odd blanket around her with hard, efficient movements. "It works as good on earth as it does in space. Reflects heat back so efficiently I damn near cook myself if I use it. I just bring it along for emergencies. If I'd known earlier how cold you were, I'd have given it to you."

Mariah couldn't have answered if her life depended on it. Even with blankets in the way, the feel of Cash's hands moving down her sides as he tucked in the odd cloth was wonderful.

Suddenly Cash shifted. His hands flattened on the floor on either side of Mariah's head. He watched her mouth with an intensity that left her weak. Slowly his head lowered until he was so close she could taste his breath, feel his heat, sense the hard beating of his heart.

"Cash . . . ?" she whispered.

His mouth settled over hers, stealing her breath, sinking into her so slowly she couldn't tell when the kiss began. At the first touch of his tongue, she made a tiny sound in her throat. A shudder ripped through Cash, yet his gradual claiming of Mariah's mouth didn't hasten. Gently, inevitably, he turned his head, opening soft feminine lips that were still parted over the sighing of his name. The velvet heat of Mariah's mouth made him dizzy. The tiny sounds she made at the back of her throat set fire to him. He rocked his head back and forth until her mouth was completely his, and then he drank deeply of her, holding the intimate kiss until her breathing was as broken and rapid as his own. Only then did he lift his head.

"You're right," Cash said hoarsely. "It isn't fair."

There was a rapid movement, then the sound of Cash climbing fully clothed into his sleeping bag.

It was a long time before either of them got to sleep.

Nine

Mariah sat on a sun-warmed boulder and watched Cash pan for gold in one of the nameless small creeks along the Devil's Peak watershed. Sunlight fell over the land in a silent golden outpouring that belied the chilly summer night to come. Stretching into the warmth, smiling, Mariah relished the clean air and the sun's heat and the feeling of happiness that had grown within her until she found herself wanting to laugh and throw her arms out in sheer pleasure.

The first days at the line shack had been hard, but after that it had been heaven. By the sixth day Mariah no longer awoke stiff every morning from a night on the hard floor and Cash no longer looked for excuses not to take her prospecting. By the eleventh day Mariah no longer questioned the depth of her attraction to Cash. She simply accepted it as she accepted lightning zigzagging through darkness or sunlight infusing the mountains with summer's heat.

Or the way she had accepted that single, incredible kiss.

Since then, Cash had been very careful to avoid touching Mariah but his restraint only made him more compelling to her senses. She had known men who wouldn't have hesitated to push her sexually if they had sensed such a deep response on her part. The fact that Cash didn't press for more was a sign to Mariah that he, too, cherished the glittering emotion that was weaving between the two of them, growing stronger with each shared laugh, each shared silence, drawing them closer and closer each day, each hour, each minute. Their closeness was becoming as tangible as the water swirling in Cash's gold pan, a transparent, fluid beauty stripping away the ordinary to reveal the gleaming gold beneath.

Shivering with a delicious combination of pleasure and anticipation each time she looked at Cash, Mariah told herself to be as patient as he was. When Cash was as certain of the strength of their emotion as she was, he would come to her again, ask for her again.

And this time she would say yes.

"Find anything?" Mariah asked, knowing the answer, wanting to hear Cash's voice anyway.

She loved the sound of it, loved seeing the flash of Cash's smile, loved the masculine pelt that had grown over his cheeks after eleven days without a razor, loved seeing the flex and play of muscles in his arms, loved . . . *him*.

"Nope. If the mine is up this draw, nothing washed down into the creek. I'll try a few hundred yards farther up, just to be sure."

Before Cash could flip the gritty contents of the pan back into the small creek, Mariah bent over his shoulder, bracing herself against his strength while she stirred through the gold pan with her fingertip. After a time she lifted her hand and examined her wet fingertip. No black flakes stuck to the small ridges on the pad of her finger. No gold ones stuck, either.

Mariah didn't care. She had already found what she sought—a chance to touch the man who had become the center of her world.

"Oh, well," she said. "There's always the next pan."

Cash smiled and watched while Mariah absently dried her fingertip on her jeans. A familiar heat pulsed through him as he looked at her. The desire he had felt the first time he saw her had done nothing but get deeper, hotter, harder. Despite the persistent ache of arousal, Cash had never enjoyed prospecting quite so much as he had in the past week. Mariah was enjoying it, too. He could see it in her smile, hear it in her easy laughter.

And she wanted him. He could see that, too, the desire in her eyes, a golden warmth that approved of everything he did, everything he said, every breath he took. He knew his eyes followed her in the same way, approving of every feminine curve, every golden glance, every breath, everything. He wanted her with a near-violent hunger he had never experienced before. All that kept him from taking what she so clearly wanted to give him was the bitter experience of the past, when he had so needed to believe a woman's lies that he had allowed her to make a fool of him. Yet no matter how closely Cash looked for cracks in Mariah's facade of warmth and vulnerability, so far he had found none.

It should have comforted him. It did not. Cash was very much afraid that his inability to see past Mariah's surface to the inevitable female calculation beneath was more a measure of how much he wanted her than it was a testimony to Mariah's innate truthfulness.

But God, how he wanted her.

Cash came to his feet in a swift, coordinated movement that startled Mariah.

"Is something wrong?"

"No gold here," Cash said curtly. He secured the gold pan to his backpack with quick motions. "We might as well

head back. It's too late to try the other side of the rise today."

Mariah looked at the downward arc of the sun. "Does
that mean there will be time for Black Springs before dinner?"

The eagerness in Mariah's voice made Cash smile ruefully. He had been very careful not to go to the hot springs
with Mariah if he could avoid it. He had enough trouble
getting to sleep at night just remembering what she looked
like bare-legged and wearing a windbreaker. He didn't need
visions of her in a wet bathing suit to keep him awake.

"Sure," he said casually. "You can soak while I catch
dinner downstream."

Disappointed at the prospect of going to the springs
alone, Mariah asked, "Aren't you stiff after a day of
crouching over ice water?"

Cash shrugged. "I'm used to it."

Using a shortcut Cash had discovered, they took only an
hour to get back to the line shack. While he picketed the
horses in fresh grass, Mariah changed into her tank suit and
windbreaker. When she appeared at the door of the cabin,
Cash glanced up for only an instant before he lowered his
head and went back to driving in picket stakes.

With a disappointment she couldn't conceal, Mariah
started up the Black Springs path. After a hundred yards she
turned around and headed back toward the cabin. Cash had
just finished picketing the last horse when he spotted Mariah walking toward him.

"What's wrong?"

"Nothing. I just decided it would be more fun to learn
how to handle a gold pan than it would be to soak in an
oversize hot tub."

Cash's indigo glance traveled from the dark wisps of hair
caressing Mariah's face to the long, elegant legs that were
naked of anything but sunlight.

"Better get some more clothes on. The stream is a hell of a lot colder than Black Springs."

"I wasn't planning on swimming."

"You'll get wet anyway. Amateurs always do."

"But it's hot. Look at you. You're in shirtsleeves and you're sweating."

He didn't bother to argue that the sun wasn't warm. If he had been alone, he would have been working stripped to the waist. But he wasn't alone. He was with a woman he wanted, a woman who wanted him, a woman he was trying very hard to be smart enough not to take.

"If you plan on learning how to pan for gold," Cash said flatly, "you better get dressed for it."

Mariah threw up her hands and went back to the line shack before Cash changed his mind about teaching her how to pan for gold at all. She tore off the windbreaker and yanked on jeans over her shoes. Without looking, she grabbed a shirt off the pile of clothes that covered her blankets. She was halfway out the door before she realized that the shirt belonged to Cash.

"Tough," she muttered, yanking the soft navy flannel into place over her tank suit and fastening the snaps impatiently. "He wanted me to be dressed. I'm dressed. He didn't say whose clothes I had to wear."

There was no point in fastening the shirt's cuffs, which hung down well past her fingertips, just as the shoulders overhung hers by four inches on either side. The shirttails draped to her knees. Yet when Cash wore the shirt, it fit him without wrinkles or gaps.

"Lord, but that man is big," Mariah muttered. "It's a good thing he doesn't bite."

Impatiently she shoved the cuffs up well past her elbows, tied a hasty knot in the tails, grabbed the gold pan and shovel and ran back to where Cash was still working on the horses.

"I'm ready," Mariah said breathlessly.

Cash looked up, blinked, tried not to smile and failed completely. He released the horse's hoof he had been cleaning and stood up.

"Next time, don't wear such a tight shirt," he said, deadpan.

"Next time," Mariah retorted, "don't leave your tiny little shirt on my blankets when I'm in a hurry."

Snickering, Cash shook his head. "Let me get my fishing rod. We'll start in the riffles way up behind the shack. The creek cuts through a nice grassy place just above the willow thicket. Grass will be a lot easier on your knees than gravel."

"Don't you need gravel to pan gold?"

"Only if you expect to find gold. You don't. You're just learning how to pan, remember?"

"Boy, wouldn't you be surprised if I found nuggets in that stream."

"Nope."

Mariah blinked. "You wouldn't be surprised?"

"Hell no, honey. I'd be dead of shock."

Her smile flashed an instant before her laughter glittered in the mountain silence, brighter than any gold Cash had ever found. Unable to resist touching her, he ruffled her hair with a brotherly gesture that was belied by the sudden heat and tension of his body. The reaction came every time he touched her, no matter how casually, which was why he tried not to touch her at all.

Unfortunately for Cash's peace of mind, there was no satisfactory way to teach Mariah how to pan for gold without touching her or at least getting so close to her that not touching was almost as arousing as touching would have been. The soft pad of grass beneath their feet, the liquid murmur of the brook and the muted rustle of nearby willows being stroked by the breeze did nothing to make the moment less sensually charged.

Mariah's own response to Cash's closeness didn't help ease the progress of the lessons at all. When he put his hands next to her's on the cold metal in order to demonstrate the proper panning technique, she forgot everything but the fact that Cash was close to her. Her motions became shaky rather than smooth, which defeated the whole point of the lessons.

"It's a good thing the pan is empty," Cash muttered finally, watching Mariah try to imitate the easy swirling motion of proper panning. "The way you're going at it, any water in that pan would be sprayed from hell to breakfast."

"It looks so easy when you do it," Mariah said unhappily. "Why can't I get the rhythm of it?"

Cursing himself silently, knowing he shouldn't do what he was about to do, Cash said, "Here, try it this way."

Before common sense could prevent him, he stepped behind Mariah, reached around her and put his hands over hers on the pan. He felt the shiver that went through her, bit back a searing word and got on with the lesson.

"You can pan with either a clockwise or counterclockwise motion," Cash said through clenched teeth. "Which do you prefer?"

Mariah closed her eyes and tried to stifle the delicious shivering that came each time Cash brushed against her. Standing as close as they were, the sweet friction occurred each time either of them breathed.

"Damn it, Mariah, wake up and concentrate! Which way do you want to pan?"

"C-count."

"What?"

"Counter." She dragged in a ragged breath. "Counterclockwise."

With more strength than finesse, Cash moved his hands in counterclockwise motions, dragging Mariah's hands along. The circles he made weren't as smooth as usual, but they were a great improvement on what she had managed alone. The problem was that, standing as they were, Cash couldn't help but breathe in Mariah's fragile, elementally female fragrance. Nor could he prevent feeling her warmth all the way down to his knees.

And if he kept standing so close to her, there would be a lot less innocent kind of touching that he couldn't—or wouldn't want to—prevent.

Yet brushing against Mariah was so sweet that Cash couldn't force himself to stop immediately. He continued to stand very close to her for several excruciating minutes, teaching her how to pan gold and testing the limits of his self-control at the same time.

"That's it," Cash said abruptly, letting go of Mariah's hands and stepping back. "You're doing much better. I'm going fishing."

"But—how much water do I put in the pan?" Mariah asked Cash's rapidly retreating back.

"As much as you can handle without spilling," he answered, not bothering to turn around.

"And how much gravel?"

There was no answer. Cash had stepped into the willow thicket and vanished.

"Cash?"

Nothing came back to Mariah but the sound of the wind.

She looked at the empty gold pan and sighed. "Well, pan, it's just you and me. May the best man win."

At first Mariah tried to imitate Cash and crouch on her heels over the stream while she panned. The unaccustomed position soon made her legs protest. She tried kneeling. As Cash had predicted, kneeling was more comfortable, but only because of the thick mat of streamside grass. Kneeling on gravel wouldn't have worked.

Alternating between crouching and kneeling, Mariah concentrated on making the water in the pan turn in proper circles. As she became better at it, she used more water. While she worked, sunlight danced across the brook, striking silver sparks from the water and pouring heat over the land.

Patiently Mariah practiced the technique Cash had taught her, increasing the amount of water in the pan by small amounts each time. The more water she used, the greater the chance that she would miscalculate and drench herself with a too-energetic swirl of the pan. So far she had managed to make her mistakes in such a way as to send the water back into the stream, but she doubted that her luck would hold indefinitely.

Just when Mariah was congratulating herself on learning how to pan without accidents, she made an incautious movement that sent a tidal wave of ice water pouring down her front. With a stifled shriek she leaped to her feet, automatically brushing sheets of water from Cash's shirt and her jeans. The motions didn't do much good as far as keeping the clothes dry, but Mariah wasn't particularly worried. Once the first shock passed, the water felt rather refreshing. Except in her right shoe, which squished.

Mariah kicked off her shoes and socks, relishing the feel of sun-warmed grass on bare feet. Sitting on her heels again, she dipped up more water in the pan. Just as she was starting to swirl the water, she sensed that she wasn't alone any longer. She spun around, spilling water down her front again. She brushed futilely at the drops, shivered at the second onslaught of ice water, and smiled up at Cash in wry defeat.

He was standing no more than an arm's length away, watching her with heavy-lidded eyes and a physical tension that was tangible.

"Cash? What's wrong?"

"I was just going to ask you the same thing."

"Why?"

"You screamed."

"Oh." Mariah gestured vaguely to her front, where water had darkened the flannel shirt to black. "I goofed."

"I can see that."

Cash could see a lot more, as well. His soaked shirt clung lovingly to Mariah's body, doing nothing to conceal the shape of her breasts and much to emphasize them. The frigid water had drawn her nipples into hard pebbles that grew more prominent with each renewed pulse of breeze.

Watching Cash, Mariah shivered again.

"You should go back to the line shack and change out of those wet clothes," he said in a strained voice. "You're cold."

"Not really. The shirt is clammy, but I can take care of that without going all the way back to the cabin."

While Mariah spoke, her hands picked apart the loose knot in the bottom of Cash's shirt. She had undone the bottom two snaps before his fingers closed over hers with barely restrained power.

"What the hell do you think you're doing?" he demanded.

"Giving my bathing suit a chance to live up to its no-drip, quick-dry advertising."

Cash looked down into Mariah's topaz eyes, felt the smooth promise of her flesh against his knuckles and could think of nothing but how easy it would be to strip the clothes from her and find out whether the feminine curves that had been haunting him were as beautiful as he had dreamed.

"Bathing suit?" he asked roughly. "You're wearing a bathing suit under your clothes?"

Mariah nodded because she couldn't speak for the sudden tension consuming her, a tension that was more than equalled in Cash's hard body.

The sound of a snap giving way seemed very loud in the hushed silence, as did Mariah's tiny, throttled gasp. Cash's hands flexed again and another snap gave way.

Mariah made no move to stop him from removing the shirt. She hadn't the strength. It was all she could do to stand beneath the sultry brilliance of his eyes while snap after snap gave way and he watched her body emerge from the dripping folds of his shirt. Where the thin fabric of the tank suit was pressed wetly against her body, everything was revealed.

Cash's breath came out in a sound that was almost a groan. "God, woman, are you sure that suit is legal?"

Mariah looked down. The high, taut curves of her breasts were tipped by flesh drawn tightly against the shock of cold water. Every change from smooth skin to textured nipple was faithfully reflected by the thin, supple fabric. She made a shocked sound and tried to cover her breasts.

It was impossible, for Cash's hands suddenly were holding Mariah's in a vise that was no less immovable for its gentleness. He looked at her breasts with half-closed eyes, too unsure of his own control to touch her. Nor could he give up the pleasure-pain of seeing her. Not just yet. She was much too alluring to turn away from.

There was neither warning nor true surprise when Cash's hands released Mariah's so that he could sweep the wet shirt from her faintly trembling body. Warm, hard palms settled on her collarbones. Long masculine fingers caressed the line of her jaw, the curve of her neck, the hollow of her throat, and the gentle feminine strength of her arms all the way to her wrists.

Too late Mariah realized that the straps of her tank suit had followed Cash's hands down her arms, leaving not even the flimsy fabric between her breasts and the blazing intensity of his eyes.

"You're perfect," Cash said hoarsely, closing his eyes like a man in pain. "So damn perfect."

For long, taut moments there was only the sound of Cash's rough breathing.

"Cash," Mariah said.

His eyes opened. They were hungry, fierce, almost wild. His voice was the same way, strained to breaking. "Just one word, honey. That's all you get. Make damn sure it's the word you want to live with.''

Mariah drew in a long, shaking breath and looked at the man she loved.

"Yes," she whispered.

Ten

Cash said nothing, simply bent and took the pink velvet tip of one breast into his mouth. The caress sent streamers of fire through Mariah's body. Her breath came out in a broken sound of pleasure that was repeated when she felt the hot, silky rasp of his tongue over her skin. Cash's warm hands enveloped her waist, kneading the flesh sensuously while his mouth tugged at her breast.

Even as Mariah savored the delicious fire licking through her body, Cash's hands shifted. Instants later her jeans were undone and long, strong fingers were pushing inside the wet denim, sliding over the frail fabric of her bathing suit, seeking the heat hidden between her thighs, finding it, stroking it in the same urgent rhythms of his mouth shaping her breast.

The twin assaults made Mariah's knees weaken, forcing her to cling to Cash's upper arms for balance. The heat and hardness of the flexed muscles beneath her hands surprised her. They were a tangible reminder of Cash's far greater physical power, a power that was made shockingly clear when he lifted her with one arm and with the other impatiently stripped away her wet jeans, leaving only the fragile tank suit between her body and his hands.

"Cash?" Mariah said, unable to control the trembling of her voice as the beginnings of sweet arousal turned to uncertainty.

His only answer was the sudden spinning of the world when he carried her down to the sun-warmed grass. Hungrily he took her mouth and in the same motion pinned her legs beneath the weight of his right thigh, holding her stretched beneath him while his hands plucked at her nipples and his tongue thrust repeatedly into her mouth.

Mariah couldn't speak, could barely breathe, and had no idea of how to respond to Cash's overwhelming urgency. After a few minutes she simply lay motionless beneath his powerful body, fighting not to cry. That, too, proved to be beyond her abilities. When Cash tore his mouth from hers and began kissing and love-biting a path to her ear, the taste of tears was plain on her cheek.

"What the hell . . . ?" he asked.

Baffled, he levered himself up until he could look down into Mariah's eyes. They were huge against the paleness of her skin, shocking in their darkness. Whatever she might have said a few minutes ago, it was brutally clear right now that she didn't want him.

"What kind of game are you playing?" Cash demanded savagely. "If you didn't want sex, why the hell did you say yes?"

Mariah's lips trembled when she tried to form words, but no words came. She no more knew what to say than she had known what to do. Tears came more and more quickly as her self-control disintegrated.

Cash swore. "You're nothing but a little tease whose bluff got called!"

With a searing word of disgust, Cash rolled aside, turning completely away from Mariah, not trusting himself even to look at her. If it weren't for his overwhelming arousal, he would have gotten to his feet and walked off. Bitterly he waited for the firestorm to pass, hating the realization that he had been so completely taken in by a woman. Again.

"I'm not a tease," Mariah said after a moment of struggling to control her tears. "I d-didn't say no."

"You didn't have to," Cash snarled. "Your body said it loud and clear."

There was a long moment of silence, followed by Mariah's broken sigh and a shaky question.

"How was I supposed to respond?"

Cash began to swear viciously; then he stopped as though he had stepped on solid ground only to find nothing beneath his feet but air. He turned toward Mariah and stared at her, unable to believe that he had heard her correctly.

"What did you say?" he asked.

"How was I supposed to respond?" she repeated shakily. "I couldn't even move. What did you want me to do?"

Cash's eyes widened and then closed tightly. An indescribable expression passed over his face, only to be replaced by no expression at all.

"Have you ever had a lover?" Cash asked neutrally.

"No," Mariah whispered. "I never really wanted one until you." She turned her face away from Cash, not able to cope with any more of his anger and contempt. Her eyes closed as her mouth curved downward. "Now I wish I'd had a hundred men. Then I would have known how to give you what you want."

Cash said something appalling beneath his breath, but the words were aimed at himself rather than at Mariah. Grimly he looked from her slender, half-naked form to the scattered clothes he had all but torn off her body. He remembered his own uncontrolled hunger, his hands on her breasts and between her legs in a wildness that only an experienced, very hungry woman would have been able to cope with. Mariah was neither.

"My fault, honey, not yours," Cash said wearily. He took off his shirt, wrapped it around Mariah like a sheet and gently took her into his arms. "I wanted you so much I lost my head. That's a sorry excuse, but it's all I have. I'm sure as hell old enough to know better."

Mariah looked up at him with uncertain golden eyes.

"Don't be afraid," he said, kissing her forehead. One hand moved down her back in slow, comforting strokes. "It's all right, honey. It won't happen again."

The easy, undemanding hug Cash gave Mariah was like a balm. With a long sigh, she rested her head against his chest. When she moved slightly, she realized that his pelt of curling hair had an intriguing texture. She rubbed her cheek against it experimentally. Liking the feeling, she snuggled even closer.

"I wasn't afraid," Mariah whispered after a moment.

Cash made a questioning sound, telling Mariah that he hadn't heard her soft words.

"I wasn't afraid of you," Mariah said, tilting back her head until she could see Cash's eyes. "It was just . . . things were happening so fast and I wanted to do what you wanted but I didn't know how."

The soothing rhythm of Cash's hand hesitated, then continued as he absorbed Mariah's words.

"Virginity doesn't guarantee sexual inexperience," he said after a time. "You're both, aren't you? Virgin and inexperienced."

"There's no such thing as a sexually experienced virgin," Mariah muttered against his chest.

He laughed softly. "Don't bet on it, honey. My ex-wife was a virgin, but she had my pants undone and her hands all over me the first time we made out."

Mariah made an indecipherable noise that sounded suspiciously like "Virgin my fanny."

"Say again?" Cash said, smiling and tilting Mariah's face up to his.

She shook her head, refusing to meet his eyes. He laughed softly and bent over her mouth. His lips brushed hers once, twice, then again and again in tender motions that soon had her mouth turning after his, seeking him in a kiss less teasing than he was giving her. He seemed to give in, only to turn partially aside at the last instant and trace her upper lip with his tongue. The sensuous caress drew a small gasp from her.

Very carefully Cash lifted his head, took a slow breath and tucked Mariah's cheek against his chest once more. She gave a rather shaky sigh and burrowed against him. Hesitantly her hands began stroking him in the same slow rhythms that he was stroking her. His chest was hot beneath the silky mat of hair, and his muscles moved sleekly. Closing her eyes, she memorized his strength with her hands, enjoying the changes in texture from silky hair to smooth skin, savoring his heat and the muscular resilience of his torso.

When Mariah's hand slid down to Cash's waist, hovered, then settled on the fastening of his jeans, his breath came in with an odd, ripping sound.

"Would you like having my hands all over you?" Mariah asked tentatively.

A shudder of anticipation and need rippled over Cash, roughening his voice. "Hell yes, I'd like it. But," he added, capturing both her hands in one of his, preventing her from moving, "not unless you'd like it, too."

"There's only one way to find out...."

With a sound rather like a groan, Cash dragged Mariah's hands up to his mouth. "Let's wait," he suggested, biting her fingers gently. "There are other things you might like better at first."

"Like what?"

"Like kissing me."

Cash bent over Mariah's lips, touched the center of her upper lip with the tip of his tongue, then retreated. He returned again, touched, retreated, returned, touched and retreated once more. The slow, sensual teasing soon had Mariah moving restlessly in his arms, trying to capture his lips, failing, trying again and again until with a sound of frustration she took his head between her hands.

The cool, course silk of Cash's growing beard was an intense contrast to the heat and satin smoothness of his lips. The difference in textures so intrigued her that she savored them repeatedly with soft, darting touches of her tongue. When his lips opened, her tongue touched only air . . . and then the tip of his tongue found hers, touched, retreated, touched, withdrew. The hot caresses lured her deeper and yet deeper into his mouth, seducing her languidly, completely, until finally she was locked with him in an embrace as urgent as the one that had dismayed her a few minutes earlier.

But this time Mariah wasn't dismayed. This time she couldn't taste Cash deeply enough, nor could she be tasted deeply enough by him in turn. She clung to him, surrendering to and demanding his embrace at the same time, wholly lost in the shimmering sensuality of the moment. When he would have ended the kiss, she made a protesting sound and closed her teeth lightly on his tongue. With a hoarse rush of breath, Cash accepted the seductive demand and made one of his own in return, nipping at her lips, her tongue, sliding into the hot darkness behind her teeth until he had total possession of her mouth once more.

Gently Cash urged Mariah over onto her back. When she was lying against the soft grass once more, he settled onto her body in slow motion, easing apart her legs, letting her feel some of his weight while he explored the sweet mouth he had claimed with rhythmic strokes of his tongue.

Mariah made a soft sound at the back of her throat and arched against Cash's hard body. She couldn't imagine what

had been wrong with her before, why his weight had frightened and then paralyzed her. The feel of his weight was delicious, maddening, incredibly arousing. Her only dilemma
was how to get closer to him, how to ease the sweet aching
of her body by pressing against his, soft against hard, fitting so perfectly.

When Cash's hips moved against Mariah, fire splintered
in the pit of her stomach. She gasped and arched against
him in an instinctive effort to feel the fire again. The sound
he made was half throttled need, half triumph at having ig-
nited the passion he had been so certain lay within her. Reluctantly, teasingly, he moved aside, lifting his body and his
mouth from hers, releasing her from a sensual prison she
had no desire to leave. Smiling, he looked down into her
dazed topaz eyes. He was breathing too fast, too hard, but
he didn't care. Mariah was breathing as quickly as he was.

"I think we can say with certainty that you like kissing
me," Cash murmured.

Mariah's only answer was to capture his face between her
hands once more, dragging his mouth back to hers. But he
evaded her with an easy strength that told her he had been
only playing at being captive before. He took her hands in
his, interlacing them and rubbing against the sensitive skin
between her fingers at the same time. When he could lace
himself no more tightly to her, he flexed his hands, gently
stretching her fingers apart. Her eyes widened as fire raced
through her in response to the unexpected sensuality of the
caress.

Smiling darkly, Cash flexed his hands once more as he
bent down to Mariah.

"Want to taste me again?" he asked against her mouth.

Mariah's lips opened on a warm outrush of breath. The
tip of her tongue traced his smile. He lifted his head just
enough to see the sensual invitation of her parted lips revealing the glistening pink heat that waited for him. He
wondered if she would open the rest of her body to him so

willingly, and if he would slide into it with such sultry ease. With a throttled groan Cash took what Mariah offered and gave her his own mouth in return.

Slowly he pulled Mariah's hands above her head until she was stretched out beneath him. Each slow thrust of his tongue, each flexing of his hands, each hoarse sound he made was another streamer of fire uncurling deep inside Mariah's body. She twisted slowly, hungrily, trying to ease the aching in her breasts and at the apex of her thighs. When Cash lifted his head and ended the kiss, she felt empty, unfinished. She whimpered her protest and tried to reach for him, but her arms were still captive, stretched above her head in sensual abandon.

Mariah's eyes opened. Cash was watching her body's sinuous, restless movement with eyes that smoldered. Breathless, she followed his glance. The shirt he had used to cover her had long since fallen aside, leaving her bare to the waist once more. Her nipples were tight and very pink. One breast showed faint red marks, legacy of his first, wild hunger.

The memory of Cash's mouth went through Mariah in a rush of fire, tightening her body until her back arched in elemental reflex. When she saw the reaction that went through Cash, shaking his strength, she arched again, watching him, enjoying the heat of his glance and the sun pouring over her naked breasts.

"If you keep that up, I'm going to think you've forgiven me for this," he said in a deep voice, touching the vague mark on her breast caressingly. "Have you forgiven me, honey?"

"Yes."

The sound was more a sigh than a word. Mariah twisted slowly, trying to bring Cash's hand into more satisfying contact with her breast, but she could not. Cash still held her arms stretched above her head, her wrists held in his left hand, her body softly pinned beneath his right hand.

"If I promise to be very gentle, will you let me kiss you again?"

This time Mariah's answer was a sound of anticipation and need that made Cash ache. Slowly he bent down to her. His tongue laved the passionate mark on her breast, then kissed it so gently she shivered.

"I'm sorry," Cash whispered, kissing the mark once more. "I didn't mean to hurt you."

"You didn't, you just surprised me," Mariah said moving restlessly, wanting more than the gentle torment of his lips. "I know you won't hurt me. And I—I liked it. Cash? *Please.*"

Cash wanted to tell Mariah what her trust and sensual pleas did to him, but he couldn't speak for the passion constricting his throat. With exquisite care he caught the tip of first one breast then the other between his teeth. The arching of her body this time was purely reflex, as was the low sound of pleasure torn from her throat when he drew her nipple into his mouth and tugged it into a taut, aching peak. When he released her she made a sound of protest that became a moan of pleasure when he captured her other breast and began drawing it into a sensitive peak, pulling small cries of passion from her.

Mariah didn't know when Cash released her hands. She only knew that the heat of his skin felt good beneath her palms, and the flexed power of his muscles beneath her probing fingers was like a drug. She couldn't get enough of it, or of him.

A lean, strong hand stroked from Mariah's breasts to her thighs and back again while Cash's mouth plucked at her hardened nipple in a sensual teasing that made her breath break into soft cries. Long fingers slid beneath the flimsy tank suit and kneaded her belly, savoring the taut muscles and resilient heat. Gradually, imperceptibly, inevitably, his hand eased down until he could feel the silken thicket concealing her most vulnerable flesh. When he could endure teasing himself no longer, he slid farther down, finding and touching a different, hotter softness.

Mariah's eyes opened and her breath came in with a startled gasp that was Cash's name.

"Easy, honey. That doesn't hurt you, does it?"

"No. It just—" Mariah's breath broke at another gliding caress. "It's so—" Another gasp came, followed by a trembling that shook her.

Mariah looked up at Cash with wide, questioning eyes, only to find that he was watching the slow twisting of her half-clothed body as he caressed her intimately. The stark sensuality of the moment made heat bloom beneath her skin, embarrassment and desire mingling. When his hand slid from between her legs, she made a broken sound of protest. An instant later she felt the fragile fabric of her tank suit being drawn down her legs until she was utterly naked. She saw the heavy-lidded blaze of Cash's eyes memorizing the secrets he had revealed, and she was caught between another rush of embarrassment and passion. He was looking at her as though he had never seen a nude woman before.

"You're beautiful," Cash breathed, shaken and violently aroused by Mariah's smooth, sultry body.

One of his big hands skimmed from her mouth to her knees, touching her reverently, marveling at the sensual contrast between her deeply flushed nipples and the pale cream of her breasts. The soft mound of nearly black curls fascinated him. He returned again and again to skim their promise, lightly seeking the honeyed softness he knew lay within.

Shivering with a combination of uncertainty and arousal, Mariah watched Cash cherish her body with slow sweeps of his hand. The dark intensity of his eyes compelled her, the tender caresses of his fingertips reassured her, the hot intimacy of seeing his hand touching the secret places of her body made her blush.

"Cash?" she asked shakily.

"If it embarrasses you," Cash said without looking up, "close your eyes. But don't ask me to. I've never touched a woman half so beautiful. If you weren't a virgin, I'd be doing things to you right now that would make you blush all the way to the soles of your feet."

"I already am," she said shakily.

A dark, lazy kind of smile was Cash's only answer. "But you like this, don't you?"

His knuckles skimmed the dark curls again, turning Mariah's answer into a broken sigh of pleasure.

"Good," he whispered, bending down to kiss her lips slowly, then rising once more, wanting to watch her. "I like it, too. There's something else I know I'll like doing. I think you'll like it even better."

Cash's fingertips caressed Mariah's thighs, sliding up and down between her knees, making her shiver. Watching her, he smiled and caressed her soft inner thighs again and again, gently easing them apart. When she resisted, he bent and took her mouth in a kiss that was sweet and gentle and deep. The rhythmic penetration and withdrawal of his tongue teased her, as did the sensual forays of his mouth over her breasts.

Soon Mariah's eyelids flickered shut as thrill after thrill of pleasure went through her. She forgot that she was naked and he was watching her, forgot that she was uncertain and he was tremendously strong, forgot her instinctive protection of the vulnerable flesh between her legs. With a moan she arched her back, demanding that he do something to ease the tightness coiling within her body.

The next time Mariah lifted, pleading for Cash, sensual heat bloomed from within the softness no man had ever touched. And then Cash's caress was inside her, testing the depth of her response, his touch sliding into her sleek heat until he could go no farther. Mariah made a low sound that could have been pain or pleasure. Before Cash could ask which, he felt the answer in the passionate melting of her body around his deep caress. The instant, fierce blaze of his own response almost undid him.

With a hoarse groan of male need, Cash sought Mariah's mouth, found it, took it in hungry rhythms of penetration and retreat. She took his mouth in return while her hands moved hungrily over his head, his chest, his back, half-wild with the need he had called from her depths. When he finally tore his mouth away from hers in an agonizing attempt to bring himself under control, Mariah's nails scored heedlessly on his arms in silent protest.

Cash didn't complain. He was asking for all of her response each time he probed caressingly within her softness and simultaneously rubbed the sleek bud that passion had drawn from her tender flesh. Mariah's quickening cries and searing meltings were a fire licking over him, arousing him violently, yet he made no move to take her. Instead, his hands pleasured and enjoyed her with an unbridled sensuality that was as new to him as it was to her, each of his caresses a mute demand and plea that was answered with liquid fire.

Finally Cash could bear no more of the sensuous torment. It was as difficult as tearing off his own skin to withdraw from Mariah's softness, but he did. The lacings of his boots felt harsh, alien, after the silky perfection of her aroused body. He yanked off his boots and socks with violent impatience, wanting only to be inside her. Shuddering with the force of his suppressed need, he fought for control of the passion that had possessed him as completely as it had possessed her.

"Is it—is it supposed to be—like this?" Mariah asked, breathing too hard, too fast, watching Cash with wild golden eyes.

"I don't know," Cash said, reaching for his belt buckle, looking at her with eyes that were black with desire. "But I'm going to find out."

Mariah's eyes widened even more as Cash stripped out of his clothes and turned toward her. Admiration became uncertainty when she looked from the muscular strength of his torso to the blunt, hard length of his arousal. She looked quickly back up to his eyes.

"If it were as bad as you're thinking now," Cash said huskily, drawing her body close to his, "the human race would have died out a long time ago."

Mariah's smile was too brief, too shaky, but she didn't withdraw from him. When Cash rubbed one of her hands slowly across his chest, she let out a long breath and closed her eyes, enjoying his newly familiar textures. Her fingertips grazed one of his smooth, flat nipples, transforming it into a nail head of desire. The realization that their bodies shared similarities beneath their obvious differences both comforted and intrigued her. She sought out his other nipple with her mouth. A slow touch of her tongue transformed his masculine flesh into a tiny, tight bud.

"You *do* like that," Mariah whispered, pleased by her discovery.

A sound that was both laughter and groan was Cash's only answer. Then her hand smoothed down his torso and breath jammed in his throat, making speech impossible. The tearing instants of hesitation when she touched the dense wedge of hair below Cash's waist shredded his control. Long fingers clamped around her wrist, dragging her hand to his aching flesh, holding her palm hard against him while his hips moved in an agony of pleasure. She made an odd sound, moved by his need. Abruptly he released her, afraid that he had shocked her.

Mariah didn't lift her hand. Her fingers curled around Cash, sliding over him in sweet, repeated explorations that pushed him partway over the brink. When she touched the sultry residue of his desire, she made a soft sound of discovery and wonder. She could not have aroused him more if she had bent down and tasted him.

Cash groaned hoarsely and clenched his teeth against the release that was coiled violently within his body, raging to be free. With fingers that trembled, he pulled Mariah's hand up to his mouth and bit the base of her palm, drawing a passionate sound from her. His hand caressed down the length of her body, sending visible shivers of response through her. When he reached the apex of her thighs, he had only to touch her and she gave way before him, trusting him.

He settled his weight slowly between her thighs, easing them apart even more, making room for his big body. She was sleek, hot, promising him a seamless joining. He pushed into her, testing the promise, savoring the feverish satin of her flesh as it yielded to him.

"Cash."

He forced himself to stop. His voice was harsh with the pain of restraint. "Does it hurt?"

"No. It—" Mariah's breath fragmented as fire streaked through her. "I—"

Even as her nails scored Cash's skin, he felt the passionate constriction and then release of her body. The hot rain of her pleasure eased his way, but not enough. Deliberately he slid his hand between their joined bodies, seeking and finding the velvet focus of her passion. Simultaneously his mouth moved against her neck, biting her with hot restraint. Fire and surprise streaked through Mariah, and then fire alone, fire ripping through her, filling her as Cash did, completely, a possession that transformed her.

Mariah's eyes opened golden with knowledge and desire.

"You feel like heaven and hell combined," Cash said, his voice rough with passion. "Everything a man could want."

Mariah tried to speak but could think of no words to describe the pleasure-pain of having so much yet not quite enough . . . heaven and hell combined. She closed her eyes and moved her hips in a sinuous, languid motion, caressing Cash as deeply as he was caressing her. Exquisite pleasure pierced her, urging her to measure him again and then again, but it wasn't enough, it was never enough, she was burning. She twisted wildly beneath the hands that would have held her still.

"Mariah," Cash said hoarsely. "Baby, stop. You don't know what you're doing to me. I—"

His voice broke as her nails dug into the clenched muscles of his hips. Sweet violence swept through him, stripping away his control. He drove into her seething softness, rocking her with the force of his need, giving all that she had demanded and then more and yet more, becoming a driving force that was as fast and deep within her as the hammering of her own heart.

At a distance Mariah heard her own voice crying Cash's name, then the world burst and she could neither see nor hear, she was being drawn tight upon a golden rack of pleasure, shuddering, wild, caught just short of some unimaginable consummation, unborn ecstasy raking at her nerves.

For an agonizing moment Cash held himself away from Mariah, watching her, sensing her violent need as clearly as he sensed his own.

"Mariah. Look at me. *Look at me.*"

Her eyelids quivered open. She looked at Cash and saw herself reflected in his eyes, a face drawn by searing pleasure that was also pain.

"Help me," she whispered.

With a hoarse cry that was her name, Cash drove deeply into Mariah once more, sealing their bodies together with the profound pulses of his release. Her body shivered in primal response, ecstasy shimmering through her, burning, bursting in pulses of pleasure so great she thought she would die of them. She clung to Cash, absorbing him into herself, crying as golden fire consumed her once more.

Cash drank Mariah's cries while ecstasy unraveled her, giving her completely to him and unraveling him completely in turn. Passion coiled impossibly, violently, within him once more. The elemental force was too overwhelming to fight. He held her hard and fast to himself, pouring himself into her again and again until there was no beginning, no end, simply Mariah surrounding him with the golden fury of mutual release.

Eleven

Mariah floated on the hot currents at the upstream end of the middle pool, keeping herself in place with languid motions of her hands. The sky overhead was a deep, crystalline blue that reminded her of Cash's eyes when he looked at her, wanting her. A delicious feeling shimmered through her at the memories of Cash's body moving over hers, his shoulders blocking out the sky, his powerful arms corded with restraint, his mouth hungry and sensual as it opened to claim her.

If only they had been able to leave the cellular phone behind, they would have remained undisturbed within Black Springs's sensual silence. But their peace was disturbed by the phone's imperious summons. It woke them from their warm tangle of blankets on the shack's wooden floor. Mariah appreciated the emergency safeguard the phone represented, but she resented its intrusion just the same.

Cash had picked up the phone, grunted a few times and hung up. Mariah had fallen asleep again, not awakening until Cash had threatened to throw her in the stream. He had taken one look at the slight hesitation in her movements as she crawled out of his sleeping bag and had sent her to Black Springs to soak. When she had tried to tell him that she wasn't really sore from the long, sweet joining of their bodies, he hadn't listened.

But she wasn't sore. Not really. She was just deliciously aware of every bit of herself, a frankly female awareness that was enhanced by the slight tenderness he deplored.

"Have I ever told you how lovely you are?"

Mariah's eyes opened and she smiled.

Cash was standing at the edge of the pool, watching her with dark blue eyes and a hunger that was more unruly for having been satisfied so completely. He knew beyond doubt what he was missing. He had sent her to the hot springs because he was afraid he wouldn't be able to keep his hands off her if she stayed in the cabin. Now he was certain he wouldn't be able to keep his hands to himself. The thin, wet fabric of her suit clung to every lush line of her body, reminding him of how good it had felt to take complete possession of her softness.

The cutoff jeans Cash wore in Black Springs didn't conceal much of his big body. Certainly not the desire that had claimed him as he stood watching Mariah.

"I'm not sure lovely is the right word for you," Mariah said, smiling. "Potent, certainly."

The shiver of desire that went over his skin as she looked at Cash did nothing to cool his body.

"Kiss me?" Mariah asked softly, holding a wet, gently steaming hand toward him.

"You're hard on my good intentions," he said in a deep voice, wading into the pool.

"Should that worry me?"

"Ask me this afternoon, when you're two hours into a half-day ride back to the ranch house."

"We have to go back so soon again?" Mariah asked, unable to hide her dismay. "Why?"

"I just got a ten-day contract in Boulder. Then I'll be back and we can go gold hunting again."

"Ten days..."

The soft wail wasn't finished. It didn't need to be. Mariah's tone said clearly how much she would miss Cash.

"Be grateful," Cash said thickly. "It will give you time to heal. I'm too damn big for you."

"I don't need time. I need...you."

The sound Cash made could have been laughter or hunger or both inextricably mixed. The water where Mariah was floating came to the middle of his thighs, not nearly high enough to conceal what her honest sensuality did to him. His former wife had used sex, not enjoyed it. At least not with him. Maybe Linda had liked sex with the father of her child.

I should be grateful that I can't get Mariah pregnant. Holding back would be impossible with her.

"Cash? Is something wrong?"

"Just thinking about the past."

"What about it?"

Without answering, Cash pulled Mariah into his arms and gave her a kiss that was hotter than the steaming, gently seething pool.

Discreetly Mariah shifted position in the saddle. After she had recovered from the initial trip to the line shack, Cash had insisted that she ride every day no matter where she was. Thanks to that, and frequent rest breaks, she wasn't particularly sore at the moment. She was very tired of her horse's choppy gait, however. Next time she would insist on a different horse.

"Are you doing okay?" Cash asked, reining in until he came alongside Mariah.

"Better than I expected. My horse missed her calling. She would have made a world-class cement mixer."

"You should have said something sooner. We'll trade."

Mariah looked at Cash and then at the small mare she rode. "Bad match. You're too big."

"Honey, I've seen Luke ride that little spotted pony all day long."

"Really? Is he a closet masochist?"

Cash smiled and shook his head. "He saves her for the roughest country the ranch has to offer. She's unflappable and surefooted as a goat. That's why Luke gave her to you. But the rough country is behind us, so there's no reason why we can't switch horses."

Before Mariah could object any more, Cash pulled his big horse to a stop and dismounted. Moments later she found herself lifted out of the saddle and into his embrace.

"You don't have to do this," she said, putting her arms around Cash's neck. "I was finally getting the hang of that spotted devil's gait."

"Call it enlightened self-interest. Luke will peel me like a ripe banana if I bring you back in bad shape. I'm supposed to be taking care of you, remember?"

"You're doing a wonderful job. I've never felt better in my life."

Mariah's smile and the feel of her fingers combing through his hair sent desire coursing through Cash. The kiss he gave her was hard and deep and hungry. His big hands smoothed over her back and hips until she was molded to him like sunlight. Then he tore his mouth away from her alluring heat and lifted her onto his horse. He stood for a moment next to the horse, looking up into Mariah's golden eyes, his hand absently stroking the resilience of her thigh while her fingertips traced the lines of his face beneath the growth of stubble.

"What are you thinking?" Mariah asked softly.

Cash hesitated, then shrugged. "Even though we'll sleep separately on the ranch, a blind man could see we're lovers."

It was Mariah's turn to hesitate. "Is that bad?"

"Only if Luke decides he didn't mean what he said about you and me."

"What did he say?"

"That you wanted me," Cash said bluntly. "That you were past the age of consent. That whatever the two of us did was our business."

Mariah flushed, embarrassed that her attraction to Cash had been so obvious from the start.

"I hope Luke meant it," Cash continued. "He and Carla are the only home I'll ever have. But what's done is done. We might as well have the pleasure of it because sure as hell we'll have the pain."

The bleak acceptance in Cash's voice stunned Mariah. Questions crowded her mind, questions she had just enough self-control not to ask. Cash had never said anything to her about their future together beyond how long he would be gone before he came back to the Rocking M and the two of them could go gold hunting again.

I haven't said anything about the future, either, Mariah reminded herself. *I haven't even told him that I love him. I keep hoping he'll tell me first. But maybe he feels the same way about speaking first. Maybe he's waiting for me to say something. Maybe...*

Cash turned, mounted the smaller horse, picked up the pack animals' lead ropes and started down the trail once more. Mariah followed, her thoughts in a turmoil, questions ricocheting in her mind.

By the time the ranch house was in sight, Mariah had decided not to press Cash for answers. It was too soon. The feelings were too new.

And she was too vulnerable.

It will be all right, Mariah told herself silently. *Cash just needs more time. Men aren't as comfortable with their emotions as women are, and Cash has already lost once at love. But he cares for me. I know he does.*

It will be all right.

As they rode up to the corral, the back door of the ranch house opened and Nevada came out to meet them. At least Mariah thought the man was Nevada until she noticed the absence of any beard.

"It's about time you got back!" Cash called out. "If I don't see Carolina more often, she won't recognize me at all."

The man took the bridle of Mariah's horse and smiled up at her. "With those eyes, you've got to be Luke's little sister, Mariah. Welcome home."

Mariah grinned at the smiling stranger who was every bit as handsome as his unsmiling younger brother. "Thanks. Now I know what Nevada looks like underneath that beard. You must be Tennessee."

"You sure about that?" Ten asked.

"Dead sure. With those shoulders and that catlike way of walking, you've got to be Nevada's older brother."

Ten laughed. "It's a shame Nevada's not the marrying kind. You'd make a fine sister-in-law."

Cash gave Ten a hard glance. Ten had no way of knowing that Mariah's gentle interest in Nevada was a raw spot with Cash. No matter how many times he told himself that Mariah had no sexual interest in Nevada, Cash kept remembering his bitter experience with Linda. It had never occurred to him that she was sleeping with another man. After all, she had come to him a virgin.

Like Mariah.

"Put your ruff down," Ten drawled to Cash, amused by his response to the idea of Nevada and Mariah together. "Nevada was the one who told me the lady was already taken."

"See that he remembers it."

Ten shook his head. "Still the Granite Man. Hard muscles and a skull to match. You sure you didn't just buy your Ph.D. from some mail-order diploma mill?"

Laughing, Cash dismounted. When Ten offered his hand to help Mariah dismount, Cash reached past the Rocking M's foreman and lifted her out of the saddle. When Cash put her down, his arm stayed around her.

"Not that I don't trust you, ramrod," Cash said dryly to Ten. "It's just that you're handsome as sin and twice as hard."

The left corner of Ten's mouth turned up. "That's Nevada you're thinking of. I'm hard as sin and twice as handsome."

Cash snickered and shook his head. "Lord, what are we going to do if Utah comes home to roost?"

Mariah blinked. "Utah?"

"Another Blackthorn," Cash explained.

"There are a lot of them," Ten added.

"Don't tell me," Mariah said quickly. "Let me guess. Fifty, right? Who got stuck being called New Hampshire?"

The two men laughed simultaneously.

"My parents weren't that ambitious," Ten said. "There are only eight of us to speak of."

"To speak of?" Mariah asked.

"The Blackthorns don't run to marriage, but kids have a way of coming along just the same." Ten smiled slightly, thinking of his own daughter.

"Is Carolina awake?" Cash asked.

"I hope not. She'll be hungry when she wakes up and Diana isn't due back from our Spring Valley house for another hour. She and Carla are measuring for drapes or rugs or some darn thing." Ten shook his head and started gathering up reins and lead ropes. "Life sure was easier when all I had to worry about was a blanket for my bedroll."

"Crocodile tears," Cash snorted. "You wouldn't go back to your old life and you know it. Hell, if a man even looks at Diana more than once, you start honing your belt knife."

"Glad you noticed," Ten said dryly.

"Not that you need to," Cash continued, struck by something he had never put into words. "Diana is a rarity among females—a one-man woman."

"And I'm the lucky man," Ten said with tangible satisfaction as he led the horses off. "You two go on up to the big house and watch Carolina sleep. I'll take care of the horses for you."

When Cash started for the house, Mariah slipped from his grasp. "I've got to clean up before Carla gets back. I don't want to get off on the wrong foot with Luke's wife."

"Carla won't care what you look like. She's too damn happy that Logan finally shook off that infection and both of them can stay on the ranch again instead of in my apartment in Boulder. Besides, I happen to know Carla's dying to meet you."

"You go ahead," Mariah urged. "I'll catch up as soon as I've showered."

He tipped up Mariah's chin, kissed her with a lingering heat that made her toes curl, and reluctantly released her.

"Don't be long," Cash said huskily.

She almost changed her mind about going at all, but the thought of standing around in camp clothes while meeting Carla stiffened Mariah's determination. As her brother's wife and the sister of the man she loved, Carla was too important to risk alienating. Bitter experience with Mariah's stepfamily had taught her how very important first impressions could be.

Putting the unhappy past out of her mind, Mariah hurried toward the old ranch house. She had her blouse half-unbuttoned when she opened the front door, only to encounter Nevada just inside the living room. He was carrying a huge carton.

"Don't stop on my account," he said, appreciation gleaming in his eyes.

Hastily Mariah fumbled with a button, trying to bring her décolletage under some control.

"Relax," he said matter-of-factly. "I'm just a pack animal."

"Funny," she muttered, feeling heat stain her cheeks. "To me you look like a man called Nevada Blackthorn."

"Optical illusion. Hold the door open and I'll prove it by disappearing."

"What are you hauling?" she asked, reaching for the door, opening it only a few inches.

"Broken crockery."

"What?"

"Ten and Diana are finally moving the Anasazi artifacts out of your way. I'm taking the stuff to their new house in Spring Valley."

"That's not necessary," Mariah said. "I don't want to be a bother. I certainly don't need every room in the old house. Please. Put everything back. Don't go to any trouble because of me."

The fear beneath Mariah's rapid words was clear. Even if Nevada hadn't heard the fear, he would have sensed it in the sudden tension of her body, felt it in the urgency of the hand wrapped around his wrist.

"You'll have to take that up with Ten and Diana," Nevada said calmly. "They were looking forward to having all this stuff moved into their new house where they could work on it whenever they wanted." He saw that Mariah didn't understand yet. "Diana is an archaeologist. She supervises the September Canyon dig. Ten is a partner in the Rocking M. He owns the land the dig is on."

Slowly Mariah's fingers relaxed their grip on Nevada's wrist, but she didn't release him yet.

"You're sure they don't mind moving their workroom?" she asked.

"They've been looking forward to it. Would have done it sooner, but Carolina came along a few weeks early and upset all their plans."

Mariah smiled uncertainly. "If you're sure..."

"I'm sure."

"Just what are you sure of?" Cash's voice asked coldly, pushing the door open. Bleak blue eyes took in Mariah's partially unbuttoned blouse and her hand wrapped around Nevada's wrist.

"I was just telling her that Diana and Ten don't mind clearing out their stuff," Nevada said in a voice as emotionless as the ice-green eyes measuring Cash's anger. "Your woman was afraid she'd be kicked off the ranch if she upset anyone."

"My woman?"

"She lit up like a Christmas tree when she heard your voice. That's as much a man's woman as it gets," Nevada said. "Now if you'll get out of my way, I'll get out of yours."

There was a long silence before Cash stepped aside. Nevada brushed past him and out the front door. Only then did Mariah realize she was holding her breath. She closed her eyes and let out air in a long sigh.

When she opened her eyes again, Cash was gone.

Twelve

Mariah showered, dried her hair, dusted on makeup and put on her favorite casual clothes—a tourmaline green blouse and matching slacks. She checked her appearance in the mirror. Everything was tucked in, no rips, no missing buttons, no spots. Satisfied, she turned away without appreciating the contrast of very dark brown hair, topaz eyes and green clothes. She had never seen herself as particularly attractive, much less striking. Yet she was just that—tall, elegantly proportioned, with high cheekbones and large, unusually colored eyes.

Mentally crossing her fingers that everything would go well with Carla, Mariah grabbed a light jacket and headed for the big house. No one answered her gentle tapping on the front door. She opened it and stuck her head in.

"Cash?" she called softly, not wanting to wake Carolina if she were still sleeping.

"In here," came the soft answer.

Mariah opened the door and walked into the living room. What she saw made her throat constrict and tears burn behind her eyelids. A clean-shaven Cash was sitting in an oversize rocking chair with a tiny baby tucked into the crook of his arm. One big hand held a bottle that looked too small in his grasp to be anything but a toy. The baby was ignoring the bottle, which held only water. Both tiny hands had locked onto one of Cash's fingers. Wide, blue-gray eyes studied the man's face with the intensity only young babies achieved.

"Isn't she something?" Cash asked softly, his voice as proud as though he were the baby's father rather than a friend of the family. "She's got a grip like a tiger."

Mariah crept closer and looked at the smooth, tiny fingers clinging to Cash's callused, much more powerful finger.

"Yes," Mariah whispered, "she's something. And so are you."

Cash looked away from the baby and saw the tears magnifying Mariah's beautiful eyes.

"It's all right," she said softly, blinking away the tears. "It's just... I thought men cared only for their own children. But you care for this baby."

"Hell, yes. It's great to hold a little girl again."

"Again?" Mariah asked, shocked. "Do you have children?"

Cash's expression changed. He looked from Mariah to the baby in his arms. "No. No children." His voice was flat, remote. "I was thinking of when Carla was born. It was Dad's second marriage, so I was ten years old when Carla came along. I took care of her a lot. Carla's mother was pretty as a rosebud, and not much more use. She married Dad so she wouldn't have to support herself." Cash shrugged and said ironically, "So what else is new? Women have lived off men since they got us kicked out of Eden."

Although Mariah flinched at Cash's brutal summation of marriage and women, she made no comment. She suspected that her mother's second marriage had been little better than Cash's description.

Cash looked back to the baby, who was slowly succumbing to sleep in his arms. He smiled, changing the lines of his face from forbidding to beguiling. Mariah's heart turned over as she realized all over again just how handsome Cash was.

"Carla was like this baby," Cash said softly. "Lively as a flea one minute and dead asleep the next. Carla used to watch me with her big blue-green eyes and I'd feel like king of the world. I could coax away her tears when no one else could. Her smile . . . God, her smile was so sweet."

"Carla was lucky to have a brother like you. She was even luckier to keep you," Mariah whispered. "Long after my grandparents took me from the Rocking M, I used to cry myself to sleep. It was Luke I was crying for, not my father."

"Luke always hoped that you were happy," Cash said, looking up at Mariah.

"It's in the past." Mariah shrugged with a casualness that went no deeper than her skin. "Anyway, I was no great bargain as a child. The man my mother married was older, wealthy, and recently widowed. I met him on Christmas Day. I had been praying very hard that the special present my mother had been hinting at would be a return trip to the Rocking M. When I was introduced to my new 'father' and his kids, I started crying for Luke. Not the best first impression I could have made," Mariah added unhappily. "A disaster, in fact. Harold and his older kids resented being saddled with a 'snot-nosed, whining seven-year-old.' Boarding schools were the answer."

Cash muttered something savage under his breath.

"Don't knock them until you've tried them," Mariah said with a wry smile. "At least I was with my own kind. And I had it better than some of the other outcasts. I got to see Mother most Christmases. And I got a good education."

The bundle in Cash's arm shifted, mewing softly, calling his attention back from Mariah. He offered little Carolina the bottle again. Her face wrinkled in disgust as she tasted the tepid water.

"Don't blame you a bit," Cash said, smiling slightly. "Compared to what you're used to, this is really thin beer."

Gently he increased the rhythm of his rocking, trying to distract the baby from her disappointment. It didn't work. Within moments Carolina's face was red and her small mouth was giving vent to surprisingly loud cries. Patiently Cash teased her lips with his fingertip. After a few more yodels, the baby began sucking industriously on the tip of his finger.

"Sneaky," Mariah said admiringly. "How long does it last?"

"Until she figures out that she's working her little rear end off for nothing."

Car doors slammed out in the front yard. Women's voices called out, to be answered from the vicinity of the barn.

"Hang in there, tiger," Cash said. "Milk is on the way."

Mariah smoothed her clothes hastily, tucked a strand of hair behind her ear and asked, "Do I look all right?"

Cash looked up. "It doesn't matter. Carla isn't so shallow that she's going to care what you look like."

Mariah heard the edge in Cash's voice and knew he was still angry about finding her with Nevada. But before she could say anything, the front door opened and a petite, very well built woman hurried in.

"Sorry I'm late. I—oh, hello. What gorgeous eyes. You must be Luke's sister. I'm Diana Blackthorn. Excuse me. Carolina is about to do her imitation of a cat with its tail in a wringer. Thanks, Cash. You have a magic touch with her. Even Ten would have had a hard time keeping the lid on her this long."

Diana whisked the small bundle from Cash's arms and vanished up the staircase, speaking to Carolina in soothing tones at every step.

Mariah blinked, not sure that she had really seen the honey-haired woman at all. "That was an archaeologist?"

"Um," Cash said tactfully.

"Ten's wife?"

"Um."

"Whew. No wonder he smiles a lot."

"Ask Diana and she'll tell you that she'd trade it all for four more inches of height."

"She can have four of mine if I can have four of hers," Mariah said instantly.

Cash came out of the rocking chair in a fluid motion and pulled Mariah close. His hands slid from her hips to her waist and on up her body, stopping at the top of her rib cage. Watching her, he eased his hands underneath her breasts, taking their warm weight into his palms, teasing her responsive nipples with his thumbs, smiling lazily.

"You're too damn sexy just the way you are," Cash said, his voice gritty, intimate, as hot as the pulse suddenly speeding in Mariah's throat. "I've never seen anything as beautiful as you were this morning in that pool wearing nothing but steam. *You watched me take you.* The sweet sounds you made then almost pushed me over the edge. Just thinking about it now makes me want to—"

"Hi, Nevada. Is that another box of shards? Good. Put them in Diana's car. Here, Logan, chew on this instead of Nosy's tail. Even if the cat doesn't mind it, I do."

The voice from the front porch froze Cash. He closed his eyes, swore softly, and released Mariah. He turned toward the front door, blocking Mariah's flushed face with his body.

"Where's my favorite nephew?" Cash called out.

"Your only nephew," Carla said, smiling as she walked into the living room. "He's a one hundred percent terror again. How's my favorite brother?"

"Your only brother, right?" Cash bent down and scooped up Logan in one arm. "Lord, boy. What have you been eating—lead? You must have gained ten pounds."

As a toddler, Logan wasn't exactly a fountain of conversation. Action was more his line. Laughing, he grabbed Cash's nose and tried to pull it off.

"That's not the way to do it," Cash said, grabbing Logan's nose gently. Very carefully Cash pulled and made a sucking, popping noise. Moments later he triumphantly held up his hand. The end of his thumb was pushed up between his index and second finger to imitate Logan's snub nose. "See? Got it! Want me to put it back on?"

With an expression of affection and amusement, Carla watched her brother and her son. Then she realized that someone was standing behind Cash. She looked around his broad shoulders and saw a woman about her own age and height hastily tucking in her blouse.

"Hello?"

Mariah bit her lip and gave up trying to straighten her clothes. "Hi, I'm—"

"Mariah!" Carla said, smiling with delight. She stepped around Cash and gave Mariah a hug. "I'm so glad you came home at last. When the lawyer told Luke his mother was dead, there was no mention of you at all. We had no way to contact you. Luke wanted so much to share Logan with you. And most of all he wanted to know that you were happy."

Mariah looked into Carla's transparent, blue-green eyes and saw only welcome. With a stifled sound, Mariah hugged Carla in return, feeling a relief so great it made her dizzy.

"Thank you," Mariah said huskily. "I was so afraid you would resent having me around."

"Don't be ridiculous. Why would anyone resent you?" Carla stared into Mariah's huge, golden-brown eyes. "You mean it. You really were worried, weren't you?"

Mariah tried to smile, but it turned upside down. "Families don't like outsiders coming to live with them."

Cash spoke without looking up from screwing Logan's nose back into place. "As you might guess from that statement, Mariah's mother didn't pick a winner for her second husband. In fact, he sounds like a real, um, prince. Kept her in boarding schools all year round."

"Why didn't he just send you back to the Rocking M?" Carla asked Mariah.

"Mother refused. She said the Rocking M was malevolent. It hated women. She could feel it devouring her. Just talking about it upset her so much I stopped asking." Mariah looked past Carla to the window that framed Mac-Kenzie Ridge's rugged lines. "I never felt that way about the ranch. I love this land. But as long as Mother was alive, I couldn't come back. She simply couldn't have coped with it."

"You're back now," Carla said quietly, "and you're staying as long as you want."

Mariah tried to speak, couldn't, and hugged her sister-in-law instead.

Cash watched the two women and told himself that no matter why Mariah had originally come to the Rocking M, she was genuinely grateful to be accepted into Luke's family. And, Cash admitted, he couldn't really blame Mariah for wanting a place she could call home. He felt the same way. The Rocking M, more than his apartment in Boulder, was his home. Only on the Rocking M were there people who gave a damn whether he came back from his field trips or died on some godforsaken granite slope.

Almost broodingly Cash watched Mariah and his sister fix dinner. With no fuss at all they went about the business of cooking a huge meal and getting to know one another. As he looked at them moving around the kitchen, Cash realized that the two women were similar in many ways. They were within a year of each other in age, within an inch in height, graceful, supremely at home with the myriad tools used to prepare food, willing to do more than half of any job they shared; and their laughter was so beautiful it made him ache.

Linda never wanted to share anything or do any work. I thought it was just because she was young, but I can see that wasn't it. She was the same age then as Mariah is now. Linda was just spoiled. Mariah may have come here looking for room and board—and a crack at Mad Jack's mine— but at least she's not afraid to work for it.

Best of all, Mariah doesn't whine.

No. Not best of all. What was best about Mariah, Cash conceded, was her incandescent sensuality. After Linda, he had never found it difficult to control himself where women were concerned. Mariah was different. He wanted her more, not less, each time. It was just as well that he was going to Boulder. He needed distance from Mariah's fire, distance and the coolness of mind to remember that a woman didn't have to be spoiled in order to manipulate a man. She simply had to be clever enough to allow him to deceive himself.

Cash was still reminding himself of how it had been with Linda when he let himself into the old house in the hour before dawn. He knew he should be on the road, driving away, putting miles between himself and Mariah. Yet he couldn't bring himself to leave without saying goodbye to her.

The front door of the old house closed softly behind Cash. An instant later he heard a whispering, rushing sound and felt Mariah's soft warmth wrapping around him, holding him with a woman's surprising strength. His arms came around her in a hard hug that lifted her feet off the floor.

Her tears were hot against his neck.

"Mariah?"

She shuddered and held on to Cash until she could trust her voice. "I couldn't sleep. I heard you loading the Jeep. I thought you weren't even going to say goodbye to me. Please don't be angry with me over Nevada. I like him but it's nothing to what I feel about you. I—"

But Cash's mouth was over hers, sealing off her words. The taste of him swept through her, making her tremble. His arms shifted subtly, both molding and supporting her body, stroking her over his hard length, telling her without a word how perfectly they fit together, hard against soft, key against lock, male and female, hunger and fulfillment.

It took an immense amount of willpower for Cash to end the kiss short of taking Mariah down to the floor and burying himself in her, ending the torment that raked him with claws of fire.

"Don't leave me," Mariah whispered when Cash lowered her feet back to the floor. "Not yet. Hold me for just a little longer. Please? I—oh, Cash, it's so cold without you."

She felt the tremor that went through Cash, heard his faint groan, and then the world tilted as he picked her up once more. Moments later he put her on the bed, grabbed the covers and pulled them up beneath her chin. She struggled against the confining sheet and comforter, trying to get her arms free, but it was impossible.

"Warm enough?" he asked. "I don't want you getting sick." His voice was too deep, too thick, telling of the heavy running of his blood. "You didn't get much sleep last night, I couldn't keep my hands off you in the pool, it was a long ride back and then you cooked a meal for twelve."

"Carla did most of the work and—"

"Bull. I was watching, honey."

"—and I loved your hands on me in the pool," Mariah said quickly, talking over Cash's voice. "I love your mouth. I love your body. I love—"

His mouth came down over hers again, ending the husky flow of words that were like tiny tongues of fire licking over him.

"I shouldn't have taken you this morning," Cash said when he managed to tear himself away from Mariah's sweet, responsive mouth. "Damn it, honey, you're nōt used to having a man yet, and you make me so hard and hungry."

"The pool must have magic healing properties," Mariah whispered, looking up at Cash with wide golden eyes. In the vague golden illumination cast by the night-light, Cash was little more than a dense man-shadow, a deep voice and powerful hands holding her imprisoned within the soft co-coon of bed covers. "And when I couldn't sleep tonight I took a long soak in the tub. I'm not sore, not even from the ride back. If you don't believe it, touch me. You'll see that I'm telling the truth. I know you want me, Cash. I felt it when you hugged me. Touch me. Then you'll know I want you, too."

"Mariah," he whispered.

Cash kissed her again and again, tiny, fierce kisses that told of his restraint and need. When she made soft sounds of response and encouragement, he deepened the kiss. As their tongues caressed, hunger ripped through him, loosening his hold on the bedclothes for a few moments.

It was all Mariah needed. She kicked aside the soft, enfolding covers even as she reached for Cash. He groaned when he saw her elegant, naked legs and the cotton nightshirt that barely came below her hips. Then she took his hand in hers and began smoothing it down her body.

He could have pulled away and they both knew it. He was far stronger than she was, more experienced, more able to control the hot currents of hunger that coursed through his body. But Mariah's abandoned sensuality disarmed him completely. When her breasts tightened and peaked visibly beneath cloth, he remembered how it felt to hold her in his

mouth, shaping and caressing her while cries of pleasure
shivered from her lips.

Even before Mariah guided Cash's hand to the sultry well
of her desire, he suspected he was lost. When he touched the
liquid heat that waited for him, he knew he was. He tried
not to trace the soft, alluring folds and failed. He skimmed
them again, probing delicately, wishing that his profession
hadn't left his fingertips so scarred and callused. She deserved to be caressed by something as silky and unmarked
as her own body.

"Baby?" Cash whispered. "Are you sure?"

The answer he received was a broken sound of pleasure
and a sensual melting that took his doubts and his breath
away. When he started to lift his hand, Mariah's fingers
tightened over his wrist, trying to hold him.

"Cash," Mariah said urgently, "don't leave yet. Please
stay with me for a little more. I—"

"Hush, honey," Cash said, kissing away Mariah's words.
"I'm not going far." He laughed shakily. "I couldn't walk
out of here right now if I had to. Don't you know what you
do to me?"

"No," she whispered. "I only know what you do to me.
I've never felt anything close to it. I didn't even know it was
possible to feel so much. It's like I've been living at night all
my life and then the sun finally came up."

The words were more arousing than any caress Cash had
ever received. His hands shook with the force of the hunger
pouring through him.

Mariah watched while Cash stripped away his clothes with
careless, powerful motions that were very different from the
tender caresses he had given to her just moments before. The
nebulous glow of the tiny night-light turned Cash's skin to
gold and the hair on his body to a dark, shimmering bronze.
Each movement he made was echoed by the black velvet
glide of shadows over his muscular body.

Cash watched Mariah as he kicked aside the last of his clothes and stood naked before her. Mariah's eyes were heavy lidded, the color of gold, shining, and they worshiped all of him, even the full, hard evidence of his desire. Still looking at him, she reached for the bottom button on her nightshirt with fingers that trembled.

Cash rested one knee on the mattress, making it give way beneath his weight. One long finger traced from the instep of Mariah's foot, up the calf, behind the knee, then slowly up the inside of her thighs. When her leg flexed in response, he smiled slowly.

"That's it, little one. Show me you want me," Cash whispered. "Make room for me between those beautiful legs."

Mariah's long legs shifted and separated. He followed each movement with dark, consuming eyes and light caresses. Slowly he knelt between her legs, watching her, seeing the same sensual tension in her that had taken his body and drawn it tight on wires of fire.

For a moment Cash didn't move, couldn't move, frozen by the beauty of Mariah's body and the trust implicit in her vulnerable position. Slowly, irresistibly, his hands pushed aside her unbuttoned nightshirt, smoothing it down over her shoulders and arms, stopping at her wrists, for he had become distracted by the rose-tipped, creamy invitation of her breasts.

Mariah made a murmurous sound of pleasure that became a soft cry as his mouth found one nipple and pulled it into a tight, shimmering focus of pleasure. When she arched up in sensual reflex, the nightshirt slid down beneath her back to her hips, stopping there, holding her hands captive. She didn't notice, for Cash's hands were smoothing up her legs, making her tremble in anticipation of the pleasure to come. When he touched her very lightly, she shivered and cried out.

"It occurred to me," Cash said, his voice deep and slow, "that something as soft as you shouldn't have to put up with hands as callused as mine."

Mariah would have told Cash how much she loved his hands, but couldn't. The feel of his tongue probing silkily into her navel took her breath away. Glittering sensations streaked through her body at the unexpected caress.

"You should be touched by something as hot and soft as you are," Cash said. He sampled the taut skin of Mariah's belly with his tongue, smiling to feel the response tightening her. His tongue flicked teasingly as he slid down her body. "Since it's too late for you to go out and find some soft gentleman to be your lover, we'll just have to do the best we can with what we've got, won't we?"

Mariah didn't understand what Cash was talking about. As far as she was concerned he was perfect as a lover. She was trying to tell him just that when she felt the first sultry touch of his tongue. The intimacy of the kiss shocked her. She tried to move, only to find her legs held in her lover's gentle, immovable hands and her wrists captive to the tangled folds of her nightdress.

"Cash—you shouldn't—I—"

"Hush," he murmured. "I've always wondered what a woman tastes like. I just never cared enough to find out. But I do now. I want you, honey. And that's what you are. Honey."

Cash's voice was like his mouth, hungry, hot, consuming. The words Mariah had been trying to speak splintered into a pleasure as elemental as the man who was loving her in hushed, wild silence. For long moments she fought to speak, to think, to breathe, but in the end could only give herself to Cash, twisting slowly, drawn upon a rack of exquisite fire.

By the time Cash finally lifted his head, Mariah was shaking and crying his name, balanced on the jagged breakpoint of release. He sensed that the lightest touch would send her over the edge. Knowing he should release her from her sensual prison, Cash still held back, loving the sound of her voice crying for him, loving the flushed, petal-softness of her need, loving the raggedness of her breathing matching his own.

At last he bent down to her once more, seeking the satin knot of sensation he had called from her, touching it with the tip of his tongue.

With a husky cry that was his name, Mariah was over-come by an ecstasy that convulsed her with savage delicacy. Cash held her and smiled despite the shudders of unful-filled need that were tearing him apart. Caressing her softly, he waited for her first, wild ecstasy to pass. Then he gently flexed her legs, drawing them up her body until she was completely open to him. With equal care he fitted his body to hers, pressing very, very slowly into her.

When he looked up, he saw Mariah watching him be-come a part of her. He felt the shivering, shimmering rip-ples of pleasure that were consuming her all over again, ecstasy renewed and redoubled by his slow filling of her body. The knowledge that she welcomed the deep physical interlocking as much as he did raced through Cash, sinking all the way into him, calling to him at a profound level, lur-ing him so deeply into Mariah that he couldn't tell where she ended and he began, for there was no difference, no sepa-ration, no boundary, nothing but their shared body shud-dering in endless, golden pulses of release.

And in the pauses between ecstasy came Mariah's voice singing a husky litany of her love for Cash.

Thirteen

Kiss me goodbye, honey. The sooner I go, the sooner I'll be back.

Mariah had heard those same words of parting from Cash many times in the five months since she had come to the Rocking M, including the one time she had declared her love. Cash's goodbyes were woven through her days, through her dreams, a pattern of separations and returns that had no end in sight. Even though Cash was no longer teaching at the university, his consulting work rarely allowed him to spend more than two weeks at a time at the Rocking M. More often, he was free for only a handful of incandescent days, followed by several weeks of loneliness after he left. Each time Mariah hoped that he would invite her to Boulder, but he hadn't.

Nor had Cash told Mariah that he loved her.

He must love me. Surely no man could make love to a woman the way Cash does to me without loving her at least a little. Carla and Luke assume Cash loves me. So does

everyone else on the Rocking M. He just can't say the words.
And is that so important, after all? His actions are those of
a man in love, and that's what matters.

Isn't it?

Mariah had no doubt about her own feelings. She had
never expected to love anyone the way she loved Cash—no
defenses, nothing held back, an endless vulnerability that
would have terrified her if Cash hadn't been so clearly happy
to see her each time he came back to the ranch.

He was gone for only four days this time and he called
every night and we talked for hours about nothing and
everything and we laughed and neither one of us wanted to
hang up. He loves me. He just doesn't say it in so many
words.

It will be all right. If he hadn't wanted children he would
have used something or seen that I did. But he never even
mentioned it.

The emotional fragility that had plagued Mariah for too
many weeks sent tears clawing at the back of her eyes. It had
been more than four months since her last period. Soon she
wouldn't be able to hide the life growing within her by leaving her pants unbuttoned and wearing her shirts out. Cash
had noticed the new richness in the curves of her body but
hadn't guessed the reason. Instead, he had teased her about
the joys of regular home cooking.

He loves children and kids love him. He'll be a wonder-
ful father.

It will be all right.

Fighting for self-control, unconsciously pressing one hand
against her body just below her waist, Mariah stood on the
small porch of the old house and stared out through the
pines at the road that wound through the pasture. She
thought she had seen a streamer of dust there a moment ago,
the kind of boiling rooster tail of grit that was raised by
Cash's Jeep when he raced over the dirt road to be with her
again.

"Are you going to tell him this time?"

Mariah started and turned away from the road. Nevada Blackthorn stood a few feet away, watching her with his uncanny green eyes.

"Tell who what?" she asked, off balance.

"Tell Cash that he's going to be a daddy sometime next spring." Nevada swore under his breath at the frightened look Mariah gave him. "Damn it, woman, you're at least four months along. You should be going to a doctor. You should be taking special vitamins. If you don't have sense enough to realize it, I do. Have you ever seen a baby that was too weak to cry? Babies don't have any control over their lives," he continued ruthlessly. "They're just born into a world that's more often cruel than not, and they make the best of it for as long as they can until they either die or grow up. Too often, they die."

Mariah simply stared at Nevada, too shocked to speak. The bleakness of his words was more than matched by his eyes, eyes that were looking at her, noting each telltale difference pregnancy had made.

"You must have decided to have the baby," Nevada said, "or you would have done something about it months ago. A woman who has guts enough to go through with a pregnancy should have guts enough to tell her man about it."

"I've tried." Mariah made a helpless gesture. "I just can't find the right time or the right words."

Because Cash has never said he loves me. But she couldn't say that aloud. She could barely stand to think it.

"The two of you go off looking for gold at least twice a month, but there's never enough time or words for you to say 'I'm pregnant'?" Nevada hissed a word beneath his breath. "If you don't have the guts to tell Cash this time, I'll take you into Cortez after he leaves. Dr. Chacon is a good man. He'll tell you what the baby needs and I'll make damn sure you get it."

Mariah looked at Nevada and knew he meant every word. He was as honest as he was hard. If he said he would help her, he would. Period.

"You're a good man," she said softly, touching his bearded jaw with her fingertips. "Thank you."

"You can thank me by telling Cash." Despite the curtness of Nevada's voice, he took Mariah's hand and squeezed it encouragingly. "You've got about twenty seconds to find the right words."

"What?"

"He's here."

Mariah spun to face the road. When she saw that Cash's battered Jeep had already turned into the dusty yard of the old house, her face lit up. She ran to the Jeep and threw herself into Cash's arms as he got out.

Cash lifted her, held her close, and looked at Nevada over Mariah's shoulder. Nevada returned the cool stare for a long moment before he turned and walked toward the bunkhouse without a backward glance.

"What did Nevada want?" Cash asked.

Mariah stiffened. Cash's voice was every bit as hard as Nevada's had been.

"He just—he was wondering when you would get here," she said hurriedly.

It was a lie and both of them knew it.

Cash's mouth flattened at the surprise and the pain tearing through him. Somehow he hadn't expected Mariah to lie. Not to him. Not about another man.

A freezing fear congealed in Cash as he realized how dangerously far he had fallen under Mariah's spell.

"Nevada wanted something else, too," Mariah said quickly, hating having told the lie. "I can't tell you what. Not yet. Before you leave, I'll tell you. I promise. But for now just hold me, Cash. Please hold me. I've missed you so!"

Cash closed his eyes and held her, feeling her supple warmth, a warmth that melted the ice of her half lie, leaving behind a cold shadow of memory, a forerunner of the betrayal he both feared and expected.

"Did you miss me?" Mariah asked. "Just a little?"

The uncertainty in her voice caught at Cash's emotions. "I always miss you. You know that."

"I just—just wanted to hear it."

Cash pulled away from Mariah until he could look down into her troubled golden eyes. The unhappiness he saw there made his heart ache despite his effort to hold himself aloof. "What is it, Mariah? What's wrong?"

She shook her head, took a deep breath and smiled up at the man she loved. "When you hold me, nothing is wrong. Come to the big house with me. Let me lust after you while I make dinner."

His expression changed to a lazy kind of sensuality that sent frissons of anticipation over Mariah's nerves. Smiling, Cash dipped his head until he could take her mouth in a kiss that left both of them short of breath.

"I'd rather you lusted after me in the old house where we can do something about it," Cash said, biting Mariah's lips with exquisite care, wanting her even more than he feared wanting her.

"So would I. But then I'd never get around to cooking dinner and the cowhands would rebel."

Laughing despite the familiar hunger tightening his body, Cash slowly released Mariah, then put his arm around her waist and began walking toward the big house. The time of reckoning and payment would come soon enough. Anticipating it would only diminish the pleasure of being within reach of Mariah's incandescent sensuality.

"I don't want to be responsible for a Rocking M rebellion," he said.

"Neither do I," Mariah answered, putting her arm around Cash's lean waist. "I tried to do as much of dinner as possible ahead of time, but Logan and Carolina decided they didn't want a nap."

Cash looked down at Mariah questioningly. "Where are Diana and Carla?"

"I'm watching the kids during the morning so Diana and Carla can work on the artifacts that keep coming in from September Canyon."

"And you're cooking six nights a week for the whole crew."

"I love to cook."

"And Diana is making an archaeologist out of you three nights a week."

"She's a very good teacher."

"And you're taking correspondence courses in commercial applications of geology. And technical writing."

Mariah nodded. "I have my first job, too," she said proudly. "The Four Corners Regional Museum wants to do a splashy four-color book about the history of the area. They commissioned specialists for each section of the book, then discovered that having knowledge isn't the same thing as being able to communicate knowledge through writing."

Ruefully Cash smiled. Despite the fact that his profession required writing reports of his fieldwork, he knew his shortcomings in that department. In fact, he had begun writing all his reports on the Rocking M. Not only did it give him more time with Mariah, he had discovered that she had a knack for finding common words to describe esoteric scientific data. He had been the one to suggest that Mariah pursue technical writing, since she obviously had a flair for it.

"So," Mariah continued, "I'm translating the geology and archaeology sections into plain English. If they like my work, I have a chance to do the whole book for them."

Cash stopped, caught Mariah's face between his hands, kissed her soundly and smiled down at her. "Congratulations, honey. When did you find out?"

"This morning. I wanted to call, but you were already on the road. I thought you would never get here. It's such a long drive. And in the winter..."

Mariah's voice trailed off. They both knew that driving to the Rocking M from Boulder was tedious under good conditions, arduous during some seasons and impossible when storms turned segments of the ranch's dirt roads into goo that even Cash's Jeep couldn't negotiate.

The difficulty of getting to the Rocking M wasn't a subject Cash wanted to pursue. If Mariah hadn't been Luke's sister, Cash would have asked her to stay with him in Boulder months ago. But that was impossible. It was one thing to go gold hunting with Mariah or to steal a few hours alone with her in the old house before both of them went to sleep in separate beds under separate roofs. It was quite another thing to set up housekeeping outside of marriage with his best friend's little sister.

The obvious solution was marriage, but that, too, was impossible. Even if Cash brought himself to trust Mariah completely—especially if he did—he wouldn't ask her to share a childless future with him. Even so, he found himself coming back to the idea of marriage again and again.

Maybe Mariah wouldn't mind. Maybe she would learn to be like me, accepting what can't be changed and enjoying Logan and Carolina whenever possible. Maybe...

And maybe not. How can I ask her to give up so much? No matter how much she thinks she loves me, she wants children of her own. I can see it every time she looks at Logan and then looks at me with a hunger that has nothing to do with sex. She wants my baby. I know it as surely as I know I can't give it to her.

But God, I can't give her up, either. I'm a fool. I know it. But I can't stop wanting her.

There wasn't any answer to the problem that circled relentlessly in Cash's mind, arguments and hopes repeated endlessly with no solution in sight. No matter how many times Cash thought about Mariah and himself and the future, he had no answer that he wanted to live with. So he did what he had always done since he had realized what being effectively sterile meant. He put the future out of his mind and concentrated on the present.

"Come on," Cash said, kissing Mariah's forehead. "I'll peel potatoes while you tell me all about your new job."

If he noticed the uncertainty in her smile, he didn't mention it, any more than she mentioned the fact that he was gripping her hand as though he expected her to run away.

Motionless, aware only of his own thoughts, Cash let himself into the old ranch house in the velvet darkness that comes just before dawn. Mariah didn't expect him. They had decided to spend the day at the ranch and not leave for Black Springs until the following dawn.

But Cash hadn't been able to stay away. He had awakened hours before, fought with himself, and finally lost. He had just enough self-control not to go into Mariah's bedroom and wake her up by slowly merging their bodies. Fighting the need that never left him even when he had just taken her, Cash went into the house and sat in what had once been Diana's workroom and gradually had evolved into an office for him and a library for Mariah's increasing collection of books.

He didn't even bother to turn on the light. He just pulled out one of the straightback chairs, faced it away from the table, and tried to reason with his unruly body and mind. His body ignored him. His mind supplied him with images of a night at the line shack when Mariah had teased him because his body steamed in the frosty autumn air. He had teased her, too, but in other ways, drawing from her the sweet cries of desire and completion that he loved to hear. The thought of hearing those cries again was a banked fire in Cash's big body, and the fire was no less hot for being temporarily controlled.

The sound of the bedroom door opening and Mariah's light footsteps crossing the living room sent a wave of desire through Cash that was so powerful he couldn't move. A light in the living room came on, throwing a golden rectangle of illumination onto the workroom floor. None of the light reached as far as Cash's feet.

"Cash?"

"Sorry, honey. I didn't mean to wake you up."

Mariah was silhouetted in the doorway. The shadow of her long flannel nightshirt rippled like black water.

"I'm here."

"What are you doing sitting in the dark?"

"Watching the moonlight. Thinking."

The huskiness of Cash's deep voice made Mariah's heartbeat quicken. She walked through the darkened room and stood in front of Cash.

"What are you thinking about?" she asked softly.

"You."

Big hands came up and wrapped around Mariah's wrists. She whispered his name even as he tugged her down into his lap. He kissed her deeply, shifting her until she sat astride his legs and he could rock her hips slowly against his body. The heavy waves of his need broke over her, sweeping away everything but the taste and feel and heat of the man she loved. When his hands found and teased her breasts, she made rippling sounds of hunger and pleasure.

When Mariah unfastened her nightshirt to ease his way, Cash followed the wash of moonlight over her skin with his tongue until she moaned. Soon her nightshirt was undone and he was naked to the waist and his jeans were open and her hands were moving over him, loving the proof of his passion, making him tighten with desire.

"If you don't stop, we'll never make it to bed," Cash said, his voice hoarse.

"But you feel so good. Better each time. You're like Black Springs, heat welling up endlessly."

Cash's laugh was short and almost harsh. "Only since I've known you."

Without warning he lifted Mariah off his lap.

"Cash?"

"Honey, if I don't move now, I won't be able to stand up at all. I want you too much."

Despite Cash's words, he made no move to get up. When Mariah's hands pushed at his jeans, tugging them down until she had the freedom of his body, he didn't object. He couldn't. He could hardly breathe for the violence of the need hammering through him. When she touched him, the breath he did have trickled out in a groan that sounded as though it had been torn from his soul.

Mariah's eyes widened and her breath caught in a rush of sensual awareness that was as elemental as the power of the man sitting before her. Her fingertips traced Cash gently again. Closing his eyes, he gave himself to her warm hands. When the caressing stopped a few moments later, he couldn't prevent a hoarse sound of protest. He heard a rustling sound, sensed Mariah's nightshirt sliding to the floor, and shuddered heavily. When he opened his eyes she was standing naked in front of him.

"Can people make love in a chair?" Mariah asked softly.

Before the words were out of her mouth, Cash's hand was caressing her inner thighs, separating them, seeking the sultry heat of her. She shivered and melted at the caress. When his touch slid into her, probing her softness, her knees gave way. Swaying, she grabbed his shoulders for balance.

"Cash?" she whispered. "Can we?"

"Sit on my lap and find out," he said, luring her closer and then closer still, easing her down until she was a balm around his hard, aching flesh and her name was a broken sigh on his lips. "Each time—better."

For Mariah, the deep rasp of Cash's voice was like being licked by loving fire. She leaned forward to wrap her arms around his neck. The movement caused sweet lightning to flicker out from the pit of her stomach. She moved again, seeking to recapture the stunningly pleasurable sensation. Again lightning curled through her body.

"That's right," Cash said huskily, encouraging Mariah's sensual movements. "Oh, yes. Like that, honey. Just... like...that."

Shivering, moving slowly, deeply, repeatedly, giving and taking as much as she could, Mariah fed their mutual fire with gliding movements of her body. When the languid dance of love was no longer enough for either of them, Cash's hands fastened onto her hips, quickening her movements. Her smile became a gasp of pleasure when he flexed hard against her, enjoying her as deeply as she did him.

He watched her, wanting all of her, breathing dark, hot words over her until control was stripped away and he poured himself into her welcoming softness. Mariah held herself utterly still, drinking Cash's release, loving him, feeling her own pleasure beginning to unravel her in golden pulses that radiated through her body, burning gently through to her soul.

And then there was a savage flaring of ecstasy that swept everything away except her voice calling huskily to Cash, telling him of her love and of their baby growing within her womb....

For an instant Cash couldn't believe what he was hearing.

"What?"

"I'm pregnant, love," she whispered, leaning forward to kiss him again.

Suddenly Cash believed it, believed he was hearing the depth of his own betrayal from lips still flushed with his kisses. He had thought he was prepared for it, thought that a woman's treachery had nothing new to teach him.

He had been wrong. He sat rigid, transfixed by an agony greater than any he had ever known...and in its wake came a rage that was every bit as deep as the passion and the pain.

"You're pregnant," Cash repeated flatly, a statement rather than a question.

He could control his voice, but not the sudden, violent rage snaking through his body, a tension that was instantly transmitted to the woman who was so intimately joined with him.

"Yes," Mariah said, trying to smile, failing, feeling the power of Cash's fingers digging into her hips. "Didn't you want this? You never tried to prevent it and you like children and I thought . . ."

Her voice died into a whisper. She swallowed, but no ease came to her suddenly dry throat. In the moonlight Cash looked like a man carved from stone.

"No, I never tried to prevent it," Cash said. "I never spend time trying to make lead into gold, either."

He heard his own words as though at a vast distance, an echo from a time when he could speak and touch and feel, a time when betrayal hadn't spread like black ice through his soul, freezing everything.

"I don't understand," Mariah whispered.

"I'll just bet you don't."

With bruising strength Cash lifted Mariah from his lap, kicked out of his entangling clothes and stood motionless, looking through her as though she weren't there. She had the dizzying feeling of being trapped in a nightmare, unable to move, unable to speak, unable even to cry. She had imagined many possible reactions to her pregnancy, even anger, but nothing like this, an absolute withdrawal from her.

"Cash?" Mariah whispered.

He didn't answer. In electric silence he studied the deceptively vulnerable appearance of the woman who stood with her face turned up to him, moonlight heightening both the elegance and the fragility of her bone structure.

She's about as fragile as a rattlesnake and a hell of a lot more dangerous. She's one very shrewd little huntress. No one will believe that I'm not the father of her baby. I could go to the nearest lab and get back the same result I got years ago, when Linda told me she was pregnant—a chance I was the father, but not much of one.

But Cash had wanted to believe in that slim chance. He had wanted it so desperately that he had blinded himself to any other possibility.

Luke would feel the same way this time. Rather than believe that his beloved Muffin was a liar, a cheat and a schemer, Luke would believe that Mariah was carrying Cash's baby. If Cash refused to marry Mariah, it would drive a wedge between himself and Luke. Perhaps even Carla. Then there would be nothing left for Cash, nowhere on earth he could call home. He had no choice but to accept the lie and marry the liar.

It was as nice a trap as any woman had ever constructed for a foolish man.

Except for one thing, one detail that could not be finessed no matter how accomplished a huntress Mariah was. There was one way to prove she was lying. It would take time, though. Time for the baby to be born, time for its blood to be tested, time for the results to be compared with Cash's own blood. Then, finally, it would be time for truth.

"When is it due."

Cash didn't recognize his own voice. There was no emotion in it, no resonance, no real question, nothing but a flat requirement that Mariah give him information.

"I d-don't know."

"What does the doctor say."

"I haven't been to one." Mariah interlaced her fingers and clenched her hands in order to keep from reaching for Cash, touching him, trying to convince herself that she actually knew the icy stranger standing naked in the darkness while he interrogated her. "That's—that's what Nevada wanted. He said he'd take me into see Dr. Chacon if I didn't tell you this time."

So that's who fathered her bastard. I should have known. God, how can one man be such a fool?

Suddenly Cash didn't trust his self-control one instant longer. Too many echoes of the past. He had known the trap. He had taken the bait anyway.

So be it.

Mariah watched as Cash dressed. Though he said nothing more, his expression and his abrupt handling of his clothes said very clearly that he was furious. Uncertainly Mariah tried to dress, but her trembling fingers forced her to be satisfied with simply pulling her nightshirt on and leaving it unfastened. When she looked up from fumbling with the nightshirt, Cash was standing at the front door watching her as though she were a stranger.

"Congratulations, honey. You just got a name for your baby and a free ride for the length of your pregnancy."

"What?"

"We're getting married. That's what you wanted, isn't it?"

"Yes, but—"

"We'll talk about it later," Cash said, speaking over Mariah's hesitant words. "Right now, I'm not in the mood to listen to any more of your *words*."

The door opened and closed and Mariah was alone.

Fourteen

It will be all right. He just needs some time to get used to the idea. He must care for me. He wouldn't have asked me to marry him if he didn't care for me, would he? Lots of men get women pregnant and don't marry them.

It will be all right.

The silent litany had been repeated so often in Mariah's mind during the long hours after dawn that the meaning of the words no longer really registered with her. She kept seeing Cash's face when he had told her that she would have a free ride and a name for the baby.

When we're married I'll be able to show Cash how much I love him. He must care for me. He doesn't have to marry me, but he chose to. It will be all right.

The more Mariah repeated the words, the less comfort they gave. Yet the endless, circling words of hope were all she had to hold against a despair so deep that it terrified her, leaving sweat cold on her skin, and a bleak, elemental cry of loss vibrating beneath her litany of hope.

Cash would marry her, but he did not want the child she was carrying. He would marry her, but he didn't believe in her love. He would marry her, but he thought she wanted only his name and the money to pay for her pregnancy. He would marry her, but he believed he had been caught in the oldest trap of all.

And how can I prove he's wrong? I have no money of my own. No home. No job. No profession. I'm working toward those things, but I don't have them yet. I have nothing to point to and say, "See, I don't need your apartment, your food, your money. I just need you, the man I love. The only man I've ever loved."

But she could not prove it.

"Mariah? You awake?"

For a wild instant she thought the male voice belonged to Cash, but even as she spun toward the front door with hope blazing on her face, she realized that it was Nevada, not Cash. She went to the front door, opened it, and looked into the pale green eyes that missed not one of the signs of grief on her face.

"Are you feeling all right?" Nevada asked.

Mariah clenched her teeth against the tears that threatened to dissolve her control. Telling Nevada what had happened would only make things worse, not better. Cash had always resented the odd, tacit understanding between Nevada and Mariah.

Nor could she tell Luke, her own brother, because telling him would in effect force him to choose between his sister and Cash, the man who was closer to him than any brother could be. No good could come of such a choice. Not for her. Not for Cash. And most of all, not for Luke, the brother who had opened his arms and his home to her after a fifteen-year separation.

"I'm . . . just a little tired." Mariah forced a smile. She noticed the flat, carefully wrapped package in Nevada's hand and changed the subject gratefully. "What's that?"

"It's yours. It came in yesterday, but I didn't have time to get it to you."

Automatically Mariah took the parcel. She looked at it curiously. There was no stamp on the outside, no address, no return address, nothing to indicate who the package was for, who had sent it or where it had come from.

"It's yours, all right," Nevada said, accurately reading Mariah's hesitation.

"What's underneath all that tape?"

"Mad Jack's map."

"Oh. I suppose they found where the mine was."

Nevada's eyes narrowed. There was no real curiosity in Mariah's voice, simply a kind of throttled desperation that was reflected in her haunted golden eyes.

"I didn't ask and they didn't tell me," Nevada said after a moment. "They just sent it back all wrapped up. I'm giving it to you the same way I got it."

Mariah looked at the parcel for a long moment before she set it aside on a nearby table. "Thank you."

"Aren't you going to open it?"

"I'll wait for...Cash."

"Last time I saw him, he was in the kitchen with Carla." Nevada looked closely at Mariah, sensing the wildness seething just beneath her surface. "You told Cash about the baby."

Mariah shivered with pent emotion. "Yes. I told him."

Without another word Mariah stepped off the porch and headed for the big house. She couldn't wait for a moment longer. Maybe by now Cash had realized that she hadn't meant to trap him. Maybe by now he understood that she loved him.

It will be all right.

Mariah was running by the time she reached the big house. She raced through the back door and into the kitchen, but no one was around. Heart hammering, she rushed into the living room. Cash was there, standing next to Carla. His hand was over her womb and there was a look of wonder on his face.

"It's moving," he said, smiling suddenly. "I can feel it moving!"

The awe in Cash's voice made Mariah's heart turn over with relief. Surely a man who was so touched by his sister's pregnancy could accept his own woman's pregnancy.

"Moving? I should say so." Carla laughed. "It's doing back flips."

A healthy holler from the second-floor nursery distracted Carla. "Logan just ran out of patience." She hurried out of the room. "Hi, Mariah. The coffee is hot."

"Thank you," Mariah said absently.

She walked up to Cash, her face suffused with hope and need. She took his hand and pressed it against her own womb.

"I think I've felt our baby moving already. But you have to be very still or you won't—"

Mariah's words ended in a swift intake of breath as Cash jerked his hand away, feeling as though he had held it in fire. The thought of what it might be like to actually feel his own child moving in the womb was a pain so great it was all he could do not to cry out.

"I can't feel a damned thing," Cash said roughly. "I guess my imagination isn't as good as yours."

He spun away, clenching his hands to conceal their fine trembling. When he spoke, his voice was so controlled as to be unrecognizable.

"I'll leave tomorrow to make the arrangements. After we're married, you'll stay here."

Mariah heard the absolute lack of emotion in Cash's voice and felt ice condense along her spine.

"What about you?" she asked.

"I'll be gone most of the time."

Tears came to Mariah's eyes. She could no more stop them than she could stop the spreading chill in her soul.

"Why?" she asked. "You never used to work so much."

"I never had a wife and baby to take care of, did I."

The neutrality of Cash's voice was like a very thin whip flaying Mariah's nerves. She swallowed but it did nothing to relieve the aching dryness of her mouth or the burning in her eyes.

"If you don't want me to be your wife," Mariah said in a shaking voice, "why did you ask me to marry you?"

Cash said something savage beneath his breath, but Mariah didn't give up. Anything, even anger, was better than the frigid lack of emotion he had been using as a weapon against her.

"Other men get women pregnant and don't marry them," she said. "Why are you marrying me?"

"I could hardly walk out on my best friend's sister, could I? And you have Carla wrapped around your little finger, too. They would think I was a real heel for knocking you up and then not marrying you."

"That's why...?" Mariah shuddered and felt the redoubling of the chill despair that had been growing in the center of her soul.

"Carla and Luke are the only family I have or ever will have," Cash continued with savage restraint.

"That's not true," Mariah said raggedly. "You have me! You have our baby!"

She went to Cash in a rush, wrapping her arms around him, holding him with all her strength. It was like holding granite. He was unyielding, rigid, motionless but for the sudden clenching of his hands when Mariah's soft body pressed against his.

"We'll be a family," she said. Her lips pressed repeatedly against his cheek, his neck, his jaw, desperate kisses that said more than words could about yearning and loneliness, love and need. "Give us a chance, Cash. You enjoyed being with me before, why not again?"

While Mariah spoke, her hands stroked Cash's back, his shoulders, his hair, the buttons of his shirt; and then her mouth was sultry against his skin. When she felt the involuntary tremor ripping through his strong body, she made a small sound in the back of her throat and rubbed her cheek against his chest.

"You enjoyed my kisses, my hands, my body, my love," Mariah said, moving slowly against Cash, shivering with the pleasure of holding him. "It can be that way again."

Cash moved with frightening power, pushing Mariah away at arm's length, holding her there. Black fury shook him as he listened to his greatest dream, his deepest hungers, his terrifying vulnerability used as weapons by the woman he had trusted too much.

"I'll support you," he said through his clenched teeth. "I'll give your bastard a name. But I'll be damned if I'll take another man's leavings to bed."

Shock turned Mariah's face as pale as salt.

"What are you saying?" she whispered hoarsely. "This baby is yours. You must know that. I came to you a virgin. You're the only man I've ever loved!"

Cash's mouth flattened into a line as narrow as the cold blaze of his eyes.

"A world-class performance, right down to the tears trembling in your long black eyelashes. There's just one thing wrong with your touching scenario of wounded innocence. I'm sterile."

Mariah shook her head numbly, unable to believe what she was hearing. Cash kept talking, battering her with the icy truth, freezing her alive.

"When I was sixteen," Cash said, "Carla came down with mumps. So did I. She recovered. So did I...after a fashion. That's why I never worried about contraceptives with you. I couldn't get you pregnant."

"But you did get me pregnant!"

"You're half right." Cash's smile made Mariah flinch. "Settle for half, baby. It's more than I got."

"Listen to me," Mariah said urgently. "I don't care what you had or when you had it or what the doctors told you afterward. They were wrong. Cash, you have to believe me. I love you. I have never slept with another man. *This baby is yours.*"

For an instant Cash's fingers dug harshly into Mariah's shoulders. Then he released her and stepped back, not trusting himself to touch her any longer.

"You're something else." He jammed his hands into the back pockets of his jeans. "Really. Something. For the first time in my life I'm grateful to Linda. If she hadn't already inoculated me against your particular kind of liar, I'd be on my knees begging your forgiveness right now. But she did inoculate me. She stuck it in and then she broke it off right at the bone."

"I—"

Cash kept right on talking over Mariah's voice.

"Virginity is no proof of fidelity," he said flatly. "Linda was a virgin, too. She told me she loved me, too. Then she told me she was pregnant. Sound familiar?" He measured Mariah's dismay with cold eyes. "Yeah, I thought it would. The difference was, I believed her. I was so damned hungry to believe that I'd gotten lucky, hit that slim, lucky chance and had gotten her pregnant. We hadn't been married five months when she came and told me she was leaving. Seems her on-again, off-again boyfriend was on again, and this time he was willing to pay her rent."

Mariah laced her fingers together in a futile attempt to stop their trembling.

"You loved her," Mariah whispered.

"I loved the idea of having gotten her pregnant. I was so convinced she was carrying my baby that I told her she couldn't have a divorce until after the baby was born. Then she could leave, but not with the baby. It would stay with me. Well, she had the baby. Then she had a blood test run on it. Turns out I hadn't been lucky. The baby wasn't mine. End of story.''

Cash made a short, thick sound that was too harsh to be a laugh. ''Want to know the really funny part? I never believed Linda loved me, but I was beginning to believe that you did. You got to me in a way Linda never did.'' He looked at Mariah suddenly, really looked at her, letting her see past the icy surface to the savage masculine rage beneath. ''Don't touch me again. You won't like what happens.''

Mariah closed her eyes and swayed, unable to bear what she saw in Cash's face. His remoteness was as terrifying as her own pain.

Suddenly she could take no more. She turned and ran from the house. The chilly air outside settled the nausea churning in her stomach. Walking swiftly, shivering, she headed for the old ranch house. The pines surrounding the old house were shivering, too, caressed by a fitful wind.

When the front door closed behind Mariah, she made a stifled sound and swayed, hugging herself against a cold that no amount of hope could banish. Slowly she sank to her knees, wishing she could cry, but even that release was beyond her.

It will be all right. It has to be. Somehow I'll make him believe me.

Slim chance, isn't that what you said? But it came true, Cash. It came true and now you won't believe in it. In my love. In me. And there's nothing I can do. Nothing!

Mariah swayed and caught her balance against the table that stood near the front door. A small, flat package slid off. Automatically she caught it before it hit the floor.

Slim chance.

Almost afraid to believe that hope was possible, Mariah stripped off paper and tape until Mad Jack's map fell into her hands. With it was a cover letter and a copy of the map.

There was no blank area on the copy, no ancient stain, no blur, nothing but a web of dotted lines telling her that she and Cash had been looking at the wrong part of Devil's Peak.

Will you believe I love you if I give you Mad Jack's mine? Will that prove to you that I'm not after a free ride like your stepmother and your wife? Will you believe me if . . .

With hands that trembled Mariah refolded the copy and put it in her jeans. Silently, quickly, she went to the workroom cupboard and changed into her trail clothes. When she was ready to leave, she pulled out a sheet of notepaper and wrote swiftly.

I have nothing of value to give you, no way to make you believe. Except one. Mad Jack's mine. It's yours now. I give it to you. All of it.

I'll find the mine and I'll fill your hands with gold and then you'll have to believe I love you. When you believe that, you'll know the baby is yours.

Slim chance.
But it was the only chance Mariah had.

Fifteen

———

The memory of Mariah's lost, frightened expression rode Cash unmercifully as he worked over his Jeep. No matter how many times he told himself she was an accomplished little liar, her stricken face contradicted him, forcing him to think rather than to react from pain and rage.

And reason told Cash that no matter how good an actress Mariah was, she didn't have the ability to make her skin turn pale. She didn't have the ability to make the black center of her eyes dilate until all the gold was gone. She didn't have the ability...but those things had happened just the same, her skin pale and her eyes dark and watching him as though she expected him to destroy her world as thoroughly as she had destroyed his.

With a savage curse Cash slammed shut the Jeep's hood and went to the old house. The instant he went through the front door, he knew the house was empty. He could feel it.

"Mariah?"

No one answered his call. With growing unease, Cash walked through the living room. Shreds of wrapping paper and tape littered the floor. On the table near the door was a typed note and what looked like Mad Jack's faded old map. Cash read the note quickly, then once more.

There was no mistake. A copy of the map had been in the package, a clean copy that supposedly showed the way to Mad Jack's mine. Automatically Cash glanced out the window, assessing the weather. Slate-bottomed clouds were billowing over the high country.

Mariah wouldn't risk it just for money. She would count on Luke to support her even if I refused.

Yet even as the thought came, Cash discarded it. Mariah had been very careful to take nothing from Luke that she didn't earn by helping Carla with Logan and the demands of being a ranch wife. That was one of the things Cash had admired about Mariah, one of the things that had gotten through his defenses.

As he turned away from the small table, he saw another piece of paper that had fallen to the floor. He picked it up, read it, and felt as though he were being wrenched apart.

It can't be true. It . . . can't . . . be.

Cash ran to the workroom and wrenched open the cupboard that held Mariah's camping clothes. It was empty.

That little fool has gone after Mad Jack's mine.

Cash looked at his watch. Three hours since Mariah had tried to seduce him and his treacherous body had responded as though love rather than lies bound him to her. Three hours since he had told her that he was sterile. Three hours since she had looked at him in shock and had tried to convince him that the baby was his. Three hours since she had looked at his face and fled.

Three hours, a treasure map, and a high-country storm coming down.

Cursing under his breath, Cash began yanking drawers open, pulling out cold-weather gear he hadn't used since the past winter. After he changed clothes, he started cramming extra clothing into a backpack. Then he remembered the Rocking M's cellular telephones. When Mariah and Cash weren't hunting gold, one of those phones was kept in the old house's tiny kitchen.

The phone was missing from its place on the kitchen counter. Cash ran out to his Jeep, opened the glove compartment and pulled out his own battery-operated unit. He punched in numbers, praying that Mad Jack's map kept Mariah out of canyons that were too steep and narrow for the signal to get in or out. Cellular phones worked better than shortwave radio, but the coverage wasn't complete. Twentieth-century technology had its limitations. The Rocking M's rugged terrain discovered every one of them.

The ringing stopped. No voice answered.

"Mariah? It's Cash."

Voiceless sound whispered in response, a rushing sense of space filled with something that was both more and less than silence.

"Mariah, turn around and come back."

There was a long, long pause before her answer came.

"No. It's my proof. When I find it you'll know I love you and then maybe, just maybe, you'll . . ."

Cash strained to hear the words, but no more came.

"Mariah. Listen to me. I don't want the damned mine. Turn around and head back to the ranch before it starts snowing."

"It already did. Then it rained a little and now it's just sort of slushy. Except for the wind, it's not too cold."

But Mariah was shivering. He could hear it in the pauses between words, just as he could hear the shifting tone of her voice when she shivered.

"Mariah, you're cold. Turn around and come back."

"No. The mine is here. It has to be. I'll find it and then I'll have p-proof that slim chances are different from none. Life's a lottery and you're one of the l-luckiest men alive.

I'm going to find your mine, Cash. Then you'll have to b-believe me. Then everything will be all right. Everything will be..."

The phone went dead.

Quickly Cash punched up the number again, ignoring the first chill tendrils of fear curling through his gut.

It can't be.

Mariah didn't answer the phone. After ten rings Cash jammed the phone into his jacket pocket, zipped the pocket shut and ran to the corral.

Slim chance.

Ice crystallized in the pit of Cash's stomach, displacing the savagery that had driven him since the instant Mariah had told him she was pregnant.

In three hours it would be freezing up in the high country. Mariah didn't have any decent winter gear. She didn't even have enough experience in cold country to know how insidious hypothermia could be, how it drained the mind's ability to reason as surely as it drained the body's coordination, cold eating away at flesh until finally the person was defenseless.

Three hours. Too much time for the cold to work on Mariah's vulnerable body. Doubly vulnerable. Pregnant.

Slim chance.

Oh God, what if I was wrong?

Trying not to think at all, Cash caught and bridled two horses. He saddled only one. Leading one horse, riding the other, Cash headed out of the ranch yard at a dead run. Mariah's trail was clear in the damp earth and slanting autumn light. Holding his mount at a hard gallop, Cash followed the trail she had left, forcing himself to think of nothing but the task in front of him. After half an hour he stopped, switched his saddle to the spare horse and took off again at a fast gallop, leading his original mount.

Although the dark, wind-raked clouds rained only fitfully, the ground was glistening with cold moisture. In the

long afternoon shadows, puddles wore a rime of ice gran-
ules left by the passage of a recent hailstorm. The horses'
breaths came out in great soft plumes, only to be torn away
by the rising wind.

Except for the wind, it's not too cold.

Mariah's words haunted Cash. He tried not to think of
how cold it was, how quickly wind stripped heat from even
his big body. Even worse than the cold was the fitful rain.
He would have preferred snow. In an emergency, dry snow
could be used as insulation against the wind, but the only
defense from rain was shelter. Otherwise wind simply sucked
out all body heat through the damp clothes, leaving behind
a chill that drained a person's strength so subtly yet so
completely that most people didn't realize how close they
were to death until it was too late; they thought they stopped
shivering because their bodies had miraculously become
warm again.

Mariah looked at the map once more, then at the dark
lava slope to her right. There was a pile of rocks that looked
rather like a lizard, but there was no lightning-killed tree
nearby. Shrugging, she reminded herself that more than a
century had passed since Mad Jack drew the map. In that
amount of time, a dead tree could have fallen and been absorbed back into the land. Carefully Mariah reined her
mount around until the lizard was at her back. The rest of
the landmarks fit well enough.

Shivering against the chill wind, she urged her horse
downhill, checking every so often in order to keep the pile
of rocks at her back. The horse was eager to get off the ex-
posed slope. It half trotted, half slid down the steep side of
a ravine. The relief from the wind was immediate.

With a long sigh, Mariah gave the horse its head and
tucked her hands into the huge pockets of her jacket. Once
in the ravine, the only way to go was downhill, which was
exactly the way Mad Jack had gone. Her fingers were so

cold that she barely felt the hard weight of the cellular phone she had jammed into one of the oversize pockets and forgotten.

I'll count to one hundred. If I don't see any granite by then, I'll get out of the ravine and head for Black Springs. It can't be more than twenty minutes from here, just around the shoulder of the ridge. It will be warm there.

Mariah had counted to eighty-three when she saw a spur ravine open off to the right. The opening was too small and too choked with stones for the horse to negotiate. Almost afraid to breathe, much less to believe, she dismounted and hung on to the stirrup until circulation and balance returned to her cold-numbed body. Scrambling, falling, getting up again, she explored the rocky ravine.

When Mariah first saw the granite, she thought it was a patch of snow along the left side of the ravine. Only as she got closer did she realize that it was rock, not ice, that gleamed palely in the fading light. The pile of rubble she crawled over to reach the granite had been made by man. The shattered, rust-encrusted remains of a shovel proved it.

Breathing quickly, shivering, Mariah knelt next to the small hole in the mountainside that had been dug by a man long dead. Inside, a vein of quartz gleamed. It was taller than she was, thicker, and running through it like sunlight through water was pure gold.

Slowly Mariah reached out. She couldn't feel the gold with her chilled fingers, but she knew it was there. With both hands she grabbed a piece of rocky debris and used it as a hammer. Despite her clumsiness, chunks of quartz fell away. Pure gold gleamed and winked as she gathered the shattered matrix in both hands. She shoved as much as she could in her oversize jacket pockets, then stood up. The weight of the rocks staggered her.

Very slowly Mariah worked her way back down the side ravine to the point where she had left her horse. It was waiting patiently, tail turned toward the wind that searched through the main ravine. Mariah tried to mount, fell, and pulled herself to her feet again. No matter how she concentrated, she couldn't get her foot through the stirrup before she lost her balance.

And her pocket was jeering at her again. It had jeered at her before, but she had ignored it.

Mariah realized that it was the cellular phone that was jeering. With numb fingers she groped through the pieces of rock and gold until she kept a grip on the phone long enough to pull it from her pocket and answer. The rings stopped, replaced by the hushed, expectant sound of an open line.

"Mariah? Mariah, it's Cash."

The phone slid through Mariah's fingers. She made a wild grab and caught the unit more by luck than skill.

"Mariah, talk to me. Where are you? Are you warm enough?"

"Clumsy. Sorry." Mariah's voice sounded odd to her own ear. Thick. Slow.

"Where are you?"

"Devil's Peak. But isn't hell warm? I'm warm, too. I think. I was cold after the rain. Now I'm tired."

The words were subtly slurred, as though she had been drinking.

"Are you on the north side of Devil's Peak?" Cash asked, his voice as hard and urgent as the wind.

Mariah frowned down at the phone as she struggled with the concept of direction. Slowly a memory of the map formed in her mind.

"And . . . west," she said finally.

"Northwest? Are you on the northwest side?"

Mariah made a sound that could have meant anything and leaned against her patient horse. The animal's warmth slowly seeped into her cold skin.

"Are you above timberline?" Cash asked.

"No."

"Are there trees around you?"

"Rocks, too. Gray. Looked like snow. Wasn't."

"Look up the mountains. Can you see me?"

Mariah shook her head. All she could see was the ravine. "Can't." She thought about trying to mount the horse again. "Tired. I need to rest."

"Mariah. Look up the mountain. You might be able to see me."

Grumbling, Mariah tried to climb out of the ravine. Her hands and feet kept surprising her. She persisted. After a while she could at least feel her feet again, and her hands. They hurt. She still couldn't claw her way out of the crumbling ravine, however.

"I can't," she said finally.

"You can't see me?"

"I can't climb out of the ravine." Mariah's voice was clearer. Moving around had revived her. "It's too steep here. And I'm cold."

"Start a fire."

She looked around. There wasn't enough debris in the bottom of the ravine for a fire. "No wood."

She shivered suddenly, violently, and for the first time became afraid.

"Talk to me, Mariah."

"Do you get lonely, too?" Then, before Cash could say anything, she added, "I wish...I wish you could have loved me just a little bit. But it will be all right. I found the mine and now it's yours and now you have to believe me...don't you?" Her voice faded, then came again. "It's so cold. You were so warm. I loved curling up against you. Better each time...love."

Cash tried to speak but couldn't for the pain choking him. He gripped the phone so hard that his fingers turned white. The next words he heard were so softly spoken that he had a hard time following them. And then he wished he hadn't been able to understand the ragged phrases pouring from Mariah.

"It will be all right...everything will be fine...it will be..."

But Mariah was crying. She no longer believed her own words.

A horse's lonesome whinny drifted up faintly from below. Cash's horse answered. He reined his mount toward the crease in the land where Mariah's tracks vanished. Balancing his weight in the stirrups, he sent his horse down the mountainside at a reckless pace. Minutes later the ravine closed around Cash, shutting out all but a slice of the cloudy sky.

"Mariah!" Cash called. *"Mariah!"*

There was no answer but that of her horse whinnying its delight into the increasing gloom.

Instants after Cash saw Mariah's horse, he saw the dark splotch of her jacket against the pale swath of granite. He dismounted in a rush and scrambled to Mariah. At the sound of his approach, she pushed herself upright and held out her hands. Quartz crystals and gold gleamed richly in the dying light.

"See? I've p-proved it. Now will you b-believe me?" she whispered.

"All you've proved is that you're a fool," Cash said, picking Mariah up in a rush, ignoring the gold that fell from her hands. "It will be dark in ten minutes—I'm damned lucky I found you at all!"

Mariah tried to say something but couldn't force herself to speak past the defeat that numbed her more deeply than any cold.

Her gift of the gold mine had meant nothing to Cash. He still didn't believe in her. She had risked it all and had nothing to show for it but the contempt of the man she loved.

He was right. She was a fool.

Sixteen

Broodingly Cash watched Mariah. In the silence and fire-light of the old line shack she looked comfortable despite the stillness of her body. Wearing dry clothes and his down sleeping bag, sitting propped up against the wall, coffee steaming from the cup held between her hands, Mariah was no longer cold. No shivers shook her body. Nor was she clumsy anymore. The pockets bulging with gold-shot rock had been as much to blame for her lack of coordination as the cold.

She's fine, Cash told himself. *Any fool could see that. Even this fool. So why do I feel like I should call her on the cellular phone right now?*

That's easy, fool. She's never been farther away from you than right now. Your stupidity nearly killed her. You expect her to thank you for that?

Flames burnished Mariah, turning her eyes to incandescent gold, heightening the color that warmth had returned to her skin.

"More soup?" Cash asked, his voice neutral.

"No, thank you."

Her voice, like her words, was polite. Mariah had been very polite since they had come to the line shack. She had protested only once—when he stripped her out of her damp clothes and dressed her in the extra pair of thermal underclothes he had brought in the backpack. When he had ignored her protest, she had fallen silent. She had stayed that way, except when he asked a direct question. Then she replied with excruciating politeness.

Not once had she met his eyes. It was as though she literally could not bear the sight of him. He didn't really blame her. He would break a mirror right now rather than look at himself in it.

"Warm enough?" Cash asked, his voice too rough.

It must have been the tenth time he had asked that question in as many minutes, but Mariah showed no impatience.

"Yes, thank you."

Cash hesitated, then asked bluntly, "Any cramps?"

That question was new. He heard the soft, ripping sound her breath made as it rushed out.

"No."

"Are you sure?"

"Yes. I'm fine. Everything is . . ." The unwitting echo of Mariah's past assurances to herself went into her like a knife. Without finishing the sentence, Mariah took a sip of coffee, swallowed and regained her voice. "Just fine, thank you."

But her eyelids flinched and the hands holding the coffee tightened suddenly, sending a ripple of hot liquid over the side. A few drops fell to the sleeping bag.

"I'm sorry," she said immediately, blotting at the drops with the sleeve of her discarded shirt. "I hope it won't stain."

"Pour the whole cup on it. I don't give a damn about the sleeping bag."

"That's very kind of you."

"*Kind?* Good God, Mariah. This is me, Cash McQueen, the fool you wanted to marry, not some stranger who just wandered in off the mountain!"

"No," she said in a low voice, blotting at the spilled coffee.

"What?"

There was no answer.

Fear condensed into certainty inside Cash. With a harsh curse he put aside his own coffee cup and sat on his heels next to Mariah.

"Look at me."

She kept dabbing at the bag, refusing to look at him.

Cash's big hand fitted itself to her chin. Gently, inexorably, he tilted her face until she was forced to meet his eyes. Then his breath came out in a low sound, as though he had been struck. Beneath the brilliant dance of reflected flames, Mariah's eyes were old, emotionless, bleak.

He looked into Mariah's golden eyes, searching for her, feeling her slipping away, nothing but emptiness in all the places she had once filled. The cold tendrils of fear that had been growing in Cash blossomed in a silent black rush, and each heartbeat told him the same cruel truth: she no longer loved the man whose lack of trust had nearly killed her. She couldn't even stand the sight of him.

Cash had thought he could feel no greater pain than he had when Mariah told him she was pregnant. He had been wrong.

"Are you sure you feel all right?" he asked, forcing the words past the pain constricting his body. "You're not acting like the same girl who went tearing up a stormy mountain looking for gold."

"I'm not," she whispered.

"What?"

"I'm not the same. I've finally learned something my stepfather spent fifteen years trying to teach me."

Cash waited.

Mariah said nothing more.

"What did you learn?" he asked when he could no longer bear the silence.

"You can't make someone love you. No matter what you do, no matter how hard you try... you can't. I thought my stepfather would love me if I got good grades and made no demands and did everything he wanted me to do." Mariah closed her eyes, shutting out the indigo bleakness of Cash's glance. "It didn't work. After a while I didn't care very much.

"But I didn't learn very much, either. I thought you would love me if only I could prove that I loved you, but all I proved was what a fool I was. You see, I had it all wrong from the start. I thought if you believed me, you would love me. Now I know that if you loved me, *then* you would believe me. So we both had a long, cold ride for nothing."

"Not for nothing," Cash said, stroking Mariah's cheek, wanting to hold her but afraid she would refuse him. "You're safe. That's something, honey. Hell, that's everything."

"Don't. I don't need pity. I'm warm, dry and healthy, thanks to you. I did thank you, didn't I?"

"Too many times. I didn't come up here for your thanks."

"I know, but you deserve thanks just the same. If my stepfather had had a chance to get rid of me, he wouldn't have walked across the street to avoid it, much less climbed a mountain in a hailstorm."

Cash's breath hissed in with shock as he realized what Mariah was implying.

"I appreciate your decency," she continued, opening her eyes at last. "You don't need to worry about losing your home with Luke and Carla because of my foolishness. Before I leave, I'll be sure they understand that none of this was your fault."

Too quickly for Cash to prevent it, Mariah pulled free of his hand, set her coffee cup aside and unzipped the sleeping bag. His hand shot out, spread flat over her abdomen and pinned her gently in place.

"What are you saying?" Cash asked, his voice dangerously soft.

Mariah tried to prevent the tremor of awareness that went through her at his touch. She failed. Somehow she had always failed when it came to love.

"I'm leaving the Rocking M. You don't have to marry me just to ensure your welcome with Luke and Carla," Mariah said, her voice careful. "You'll always have a home with them."

"So will you." Cash's eyes searched hers, looking for the emotions that he had always found in her before, praying that he hadn't raced up the mountain only to lose her after all. "You'll have a home. Always. I'll make sure of it."

Mariah closed her eyes again and fought against the emotions that were just beneath her frozen surface.

"That's very generous of you," Mariah said, her voice husky with restraint. "But it's not necessary." She tried to get up, but Cash's big hand still held her captive. "May I get up now?" she asked politely.

"Not yet."

Cash's big hand moved subtly, almost caressingly. He couldn't free Mariah. Not yet. If he let her go he would never see her again. He clenched his jaw against the pain of an understanding that had come too late. He tried to speak, found it impossible, and fought in silence to control his emotions. When he could speak again, his voice was a harsh rasp.

"Look at me, Mariah."

She shook her head, refusing him.

"Do you hate me so much?" he asked in a low, constrained voice.

Shocked, Mariah opened her eyes.

"You have every right," Cash continued. "I damn near killed you. But if you think I'm going to let you go, you're as big a fool as I was. You loved me once. You can learn to love me again." He shifted his weight onto his knees as he bent down to her. "Forgive me, Mariah," he whispered against her lips. "Love me again. I need you so much it terrifies me."

Mariah would have spoken then, but he had taken her breath. Trembling, she opened her lips beneath his, inviting his kiss. She sensed the tremor that ripped through him, felt the sudden iron power of his arms, tasted the heat and hunger of his mouth. The world shifted until she was lying down and he was with her, surrounding her with a vital warmth that was so glorious she wept silently with the sheer beauty of it.

Suddenly Cash's arms tightened and he went very still.

"Cash? What's wrong?"

"Didn't you feel it?" he asked, his voice strained.

"What?"

"Our baby." Cash closed his eyes but could not entirely conceal the glitter of his tears. "My God," he breathed. *"I felt our baby move."*

"Are you certain?"

His eyes opened. He smiled down at Mariah, sensing the question she hadn't asked. He kissed her gently once, twice, then again and again, whispering between each kiss.

"I'm very certain."

"Cash?" she whispered, her eyes blazing with hope.

"I love you, Mariah," he said, kissing her hand, holding it against his heart. "I love you so damned much."

Laughing, crying, holding on to Cash, Mariah absorbed his whispered words and his warmth, his trust and his love, and gave her own in return. He held her, loving her with his hands and his voice and his body, until finally they lay at peace in each other's arms, so close that they breathed the same scents, shared the same warmth ... and felt the butterfly wings of new life fluttering softly in Mariah's womb.

Cash's big hand rested lightly over Mariah's womb.

"Go to sleep, little baby. Mom and Dad are right here. Everything is all right."

* * * * *

Look for Nevada Blackthorn's story next month in WARRIOR #631.

SILHOUETTE'S "BIG WIN"
SWEEPSTAKES RULES & REGULATIONS
NO PURCHASE NECESSARY TO ENTER OR RECEIVE A PRIZE

1. To enter the Sweepstakes and join the Reader Service, scratch off the metallic strips on all your BIG WIN tickets #1–#6. This will reveal the potential values for each Sweepstakes entry number, the number of free book(s) you will receive and your free bonus gift as part of our Reader Service. If you do not wish to take advantage of our Reader Service but wish to enter the Sweepstakes only, scratch off the metallic strips on your BIG WIN tickets #1–#4. Return your entire sheet of tickets intact. Incomplete and/or inaccurate entries are ineligible for that section or sections of prizes. Torstar Corp. and its affiliates are not responsible for mutilated or unreadable entries or inadvertent printing errors. Mechanically reproduced entries are null and void.

2. Whether you take advantage of this offer or not, on or about April 30, 1992, at the offices of Marden-Kane Inc., Lake Success, NY, your Sweepstakes numbers will be compared against the list of winning numbers generated at random by the computer. However, prizes will only be awarded to individuals who have entered the Sweepstakes. In the event that all prizes are not claimed, a random drawing will be held from all qualified entries received from March 30, 1990 to March 31, 1992, to award all unclaimed prizes. All cash prizes (Grand to Sixth), will be mailed to the winners and are payable by check in U.S. funds. Seventh prize will be shipped to winners via third-class mail. These prizes are in addition to any free, surprise or mystery gifts that might be offered. Versions of this Sweepstakes with different prizes of approximate equal value may appear at retail outlets or in other mailings by Torstar Corp. and its affiliates.

3. The following prizes are awarded in this sweepstakes: ★ Grand Prize (1) $1,000,000; First Prize (1) $25,000; Second Prize (1) $10,000; Third Prize (5) $5,000; Fourth Prize (10) $1,000; Fifth Prize (100) $250; Sixth Prize (2,500) $10; ★ ★ Seventh Prize (6,000) $12.95 ARV.

   ★ This presentation offers a Grand Prize of a $1,000,000 annuity. Winner will receive $33,333.33 a year for 30 years without interest totalling $1,000,000.

   ★ ★ Seventh Prize: A fully illustrated hardcover book published by Torstar Corp. Approximate Retail Value of the book is $12.95.

   Entrants may cancel the Reader Service at anytime without cost or obligation to buy (see details in center insert card).

4. This Sweepstakes is being conducted under the supervision of an independent judging organization. By entering this Sweepstakes, each entrant accepts and agrees to be bound by these rules and the decisions of the judges, which shall be final and binding. Odds of winning in the random drawing are dependent upon the total number of entries received. Taxes, if any, are the sole responsibility of the winners. Prizes are nontransferable. All entries must be received at the address printed on the reply card and must be postmarked no later than 12:00 MIDNIGHT on March 31, 1992. The drawing for all unclaimed Sweepstakes prizes will take place on May 30, 1992, at 12:00 NOON, at the offices of Marden-Kane, Inc., Lake Success, New York.

5. This offer is open to residents of the U.S., the United Kingdom, France and Canada, 18 years or older, except employees and their immediate family members of Torstar Corp., its affiliates, subsidiaries, and all the other agencies, entities and persons connected with the use, marketing or conduct of this Sweepstakes. All Federal, State, Provincial and local laws apply. Void wherever prohibited or restricted by law. Any litigation within the Province of Quebec respecting the conduct and awarding of a prize in this publicity contest must be submitted to the Régie des Loteries et Courses du Québec.

6. Winners will be notified by mail and may be required to execute an affidavit of eligibility and release, which must be returned within 14 days after notification or an alternate winner will be selected. Canadian winners will be required to correctly answer an arithmetical skill-testing question administered by mail, which must be returned within a limited time. Winners consent to the use of their names, photographs and/or likenesses for advertising and publicity in conjunction with this and similar promotions without additional compensation. For a list of our major prize winners, send a stamped, self-addressed ENVELOPE to: WINNERS LIST, c/o Marden-Kane, Inc., P.O. Box 701, SAYREVILLE, NJ 08871. Requests for Winners Lists will be fulfilled after the May 30, 1992 drawing date.

If Sweepstakes entry form is missing, please print your name and address on a 3" ×5" piece of plain paper and send to:

In the U.S.	In Canada
Silhouette's "BIG WIN" Sweepstakes	Silhouette's "BIG WIN" Sweepstakes
3010 Walden Ave.	P.O. Box 609
P.O. Box 1867	Fort Erie, Ontario
Buffalo, NY 14269-1867	L2A 5X3

Offer limited to one per household.

© 1991 Harlequin Enterprises Limited   Printed in the U.S.A.

LTY-S391D

SILHOUETTE·INTIMATE·MOMENTS®

NORA ROBERTS
Night Shadow

People all over the city of Urbana were asking, Who was that masked man?

Assistant district attorney Deborah O'Roarke was the first to learn his secret identity . . . and her life would never be the same.

The stories of the lives and loves of the O'Roarke sisters began in January 1991 with NIGHT SHIFT, Silhouette Intimate Moments #365. And if you want to know more about Deborah and the man behind the mask, look for NIGHT SHADOW, Silhouette Intimate Moments #373.

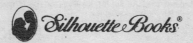

Silhouette Books®